mon

CHEYENNE'S RAINBOW WARRIOR

CHEYENNE'S RAINBOW WARRIOR

•

Jane McBride Choate

AVALON BOOKS
THOMAS BOUREGY AND COMPANY, INC.
401 LAFAYETTE STREET
NEW YORK, NEW YORK 10003

PRINTED IN THE UNITED STATES OF AMERICA
ON ACID-FREE PAPER
BY HADDON CRAFTSMEN, BLOOMSBURG, PENNSYLVANIA

To my Aunt Florence, who can always make me laugh

Chapter One

The pounding of hooves pummeling the drought-hardened ground had Cheyenne turning in her saddle. She watched as two of her men rode up. They wore the same rueful expressions that shadowed her own face.

"Sorry, Boss," Hank Summers said, taking off his hat and wiping his forehead with a sweat-stained kerchief. "No luck."

Ten more sheep were down due to a pack of wolves. They'd been hunting the pack for the last two days and had yet to catch a glimpse of them. Two years ago, she'd added sheep to her operation, since the fluctuating price of beef made cattle ranching alone a risky proposition.

1

Cheyenne tilted back her hat and squinted into the distance, looking for a hint of rain. ''It's hot enough to fry an egg on a rock.''

''It's supposed to get hotter tomorrow,'' the second man, Quinn Harding, said, uncapping his canteen. He took a long swallow, the water dribbling over his whiskered chin and down his chicken-skin neck.

Cheyenne opened her own canteen and let the water trickle down her throat. The lukewarm water tasted of metal, but it was still the sweetest thing she could ever remember drinking. She knew the dangers of dehydration.

''So what else is new?'' Besides the fact that some bureaucrat was due to arrive tomorrow to start marking trails for city folk wanting to experience the great outdoors, and she was supposed to show him around. Besides the fact that there were always too few hours in the day to do everything that needed to be done to keep a ranch the size of hers going. Besides the fact that there was never enough money.

She pinched the bridge of her nose to relieve some of the pressure she felt mounting. A familiar tension gnawed at the back of her neck. Out of long habit, she ignored it.

She watched as the men exchanged wary looks. ''Sorry,'' she said. Whatever her problems, she didn't have the right to take it out on them. "We'll try again."

Hank touched the brim of his hat. "Sure thing, Boss."

Cheyenne knew they were waiting for her, but she waved them on. She needed some time alone right now. "I'll see you back at the ranch in a couple of hours. Tell Uncle Charlie not to worry."

She watched as they rode off until they were no more than a puff of dust in the distance. Heat shimmered in waves, causing her to pull her hat down to shade her eyes.

Taffy neighed, an impatient reminder that she didn't like the inactivity.

"Okay, girl," Cheyenne murmured and slapped Taffy gently on the flank. "Come on." She settled her hat more firmly on her head, nudged the mare with her heels, and started off. She turned toward the west, to the foothills that ringed her land.

The air thinned as they climbed. She picked their way carefully, mindful that the dry ground was pockmarked with cavities and fissures. A wrong step, and she and Taffy could both go down. She patted Taffy's neck, reining her in slightly. The little mare didn't like slowing the pace, even when the going got rough. She was as sassy as they came, and twice as game.

"Settle down, girl. We're in no hurry."

At the first crest, Cheyenne pulled up to look over the valley below. *Her land.* The words never failed to thrill her, nor to remind her of what was entrusted to her. She spread her arms wide to encompass the vastness before her.

Scorched by the late summer heat and scarred by the wind that had carved jagged ridges and deep gullies into it, the land was as harsh as it was beautiful. It was an exacting taskmaster. It demanded backbreaking work, sweat, and every ounce of energy she had to give. And then some.

Uncle Charlie had taught her that the land was a trust, passed down from one generation to the next. No one could own it, he'd told her more than once, only care for it and preserve that heritage for the next generation. The land was so tied to her uncle that she couldn't think of one without thinking of the other.

She loved both of them. Without reservation. Without the uncertainty that colored almost every other aspect of her life. Her people had lived and died here; it was her heritage as well as her legacy.

"You have the spirit of your ancestors running through your veins," Uncle Charlie had told her long ago. "The kind of spirit that makes you fight when your land is threatened."

She hadn't understood what he'd meant at the

time. Her great-uncle often talked in riddles. But she'd taken his words to heart.

He'd made sure she respected the land as well as loved it. She remembered a picnic when he'd taken her to one of the canyons that cut through the ranch. As they prepared to leave, she had carelessly tossed the trash to the ground. Quietly, her uncle had cleaned up the area, leaving it as pristine as when they came. He'd never said a word to her about the incident. He hadn't needed to.

She understood now.

The land, no more now than scorched earth, pulled at her, as it always did. She itched to touch it, run her fingers through it, get her hands dirty with it. She dismounted, hunkered over, and picked up a handful of dirt. It sifted through her fingers, so parched that it literally begged for water.

To the east, the riverbed was as dry as the monthly reports she was forced to fill out. Other summers, wildflowers had covered the hillsides with a bright blanket of color. Now they were only a memory. Sheep dotted the high meadows, patches of gray and white against the summer-yellowed grass. She grazed the cattle on a pasture nearer to the homestead.

When snow came, they'd drive the cattle down to the low meadow. An early blizzard could wipe out a herd grazing in the high country. The sheep could tolerate the harsher weather. There was time yet, she thought.

She had learned to interpret nature's signs. A lifetime of ranch work had taught her how to *feel* the changes coming. It was a good life. She couldn't imagine living anywhere else.

How could anyone prefer the suffocation of the city, she wondered, where a person felt smothered with too many people, too many things? She recalled a recent trip to Laramie, the streets choked with cars and indignant drivers, buildings a gaudy parody of nature's own skyscraping mountains, and houses bunched close together with scarcely a slice of sky between them.

She could hardly take a step without bumping into someone. It was a pretty enough city, she'd supposed, if you liked all the noise and confusion. The sheer number of people, where everyone seemed in some desperate rush to get somewhere other than where they were, had made her yearn for the quiet, lazy pace of home and the clean air that was perfumed by the scent of pines rather than of exhaust fumes.

Of course, a city dweller might see things differently, might not feel the tug of the land, the freedom of the open range.

When the time had come for her to go to college,

she'd balked at the idea, fighting it with every breath and every argument she could summon.

In the end, Uncle Charlie had had his way. ''Learn the white man's ways, Daughter,'' he'd said. ''Then come back and show us how to use your knowledge to make a better life for our people.''

Cheyenne had crammed four years of college into three, worked two part-time jobs to support herself and have enough money to send some home each month, and waited for the day she could return to the land she loved.

They'd been hard years. She hadn't had time for the parties and dates that most of her friends considered so important. Work, study, and more work. None of that had mattered, though. The only thing that had mattered was coming home.

Out of habit, she scanned the sky, hoping the few clouds she saw there meant rain. A rancher spent a good part of her life praying about rain. Too little meant drought; too much, flooding. Land baked hard by the sun for three months needed a gentle soaking. Too frequently, late summer storms pounded the ground ruthlessly. The shriveled earth had no chance to absorb the moisture and flooded the riverbeds. Many a rancher had lost stock due to flash floods. Many more lost stock to the effects of dehydration.

Summer heat had sapped the land dry and the energy from all who made their living from it. Her own was fraying, along with her temper. As the temperature had soared, her appetite had all but disappeared.

She'd dropped five pounds in the last two weeks and had cinched her belt on the last notch, hoping Uncle Charlie hadn't noticed. He rarely missed a thing, but his heart attack six months ago had changed things.

She'd been forced to bring him inside, to take him away from the work and the land he loved. That had nearly broken her heart. Better that, though, she reminded herself, than to lose him altogether. The fear that another attack would rob her of the only family she had left never fully left her.

She headed Taffy home, letting the mare set the pace once they were beyond the rough stretch. The dry wind whipped through her hair as Taffy's nimble legs ate up the ground.

The ride had done them both good.

Back at Sweet Water Ranch, she took her time in wiping down Taffy, sweet-talking the little mare, the nonsense words soothing them both. She was putting off going inside; she acknowledged it. And still she stalled.

Uncle Charlie found her stealing into the kitchen. ''I made stew.''

She was about to say she wasn't hungry, when she thought better of it. She couldn't disappoint her uncle. Taking over the cooking and other household chores was his way of helping out. She knew he chafed at the inactivity of being confined inside when his world had always been outside, among the animals.

''Thanks. I'd like that.''

He nodded approvingly. ''You wash up.''

Cheyenne watched as he headed to the stove, her gaze softening. Uncle Charlie was the closest thing to a father she'd ever had. He'd helped Cheyenne with her homework, tended her when she was sick, and scolded her when she'd deserved it. She smiled, thinking he wasn't above giving her a scolding even now when he thought she needed it.

Cheyenne had been only five when her father had left, but she hadn't forgotten her mother's despair. It was then that Uncle Charlie, her mother's uncle, had come to live with them. He'd been the glue that held them all together during those first terrible months after her father's desertion.

Her mother had blossomed under her uncle's love and support. Slowly, the wounds had started to heal, and the smiling woman who Cheyenne remembered reappeared. It had taken her several years to get over her mother's death seven years later. She shook away the sadness and reminded herself of her promise to remember the good times.

Uncle Charlie ladled stew into bowls and set them on the table. Fried bread and tomatoes from the kitchen garden completed the meal.

She picked at her food, too tired to do much more than push it around. Only her uncle's steady gaze made her take a few bites, and then a few more. He kept up a steady stream of conversation about the drought and the new bull they'd bought at the last auction, until she finished. Surprised, she looked down at her empty bowl and grinned. He knew what she needed better than she did herself.

She started to clear away the dishes when Uncle Charlie changed the subject. ''He'll be here tomorrow.''

Deliberately obtuse, she asked, ''Who?''

Her uncle gave her a reproving look but ignored the question. ''He'll be expecting a place to stay.''

''He'll get it,'' she said shortly, her good mood evaporating. And he would, she promised herself. Giving hospitality to a *bureaucrat*—she mentally sneered the word—wasn't high on her list, but she'd given her word, and she'd keep it.

''We need him,'' Uncle Charlie said in the same quiet voice.

''You mean we need the money he'll bring.''

Volunteering their place to be headquarters for

the surveyor had been Uncle Charlie's idea. She'd agreed because she knew he was trying to help with the bills. And the money the Conservancy for Parks and Forests had agreed to pay would come in handy. However much she wanted to, there was no denying that any influx of cash would be welcome.

He lifted a shoulder in response. "I had a vision. The spirits have sent him to us."

Cheyenne frowned. She knew better than to question her uncle's visions. They frequently held an otherworldly quality, but they had proved themselves true too often to be ignored.

"I'll behave," she said.

He smiled. "I know, Smiling Sun," he said, using the Shoshone name for her. "You are a good daughter." As he'd known they would, the words brought a quick smile to her face.

She hugged him, a fierce, tight embrace that left them both clinging to each other. "And you are my father." *In every way that mattered,* she thought. Uncle Charlie was the only father she remembered.

"I'll see to the cabin first thing tomorrow," she promised.

He patted her shoulder. "You will see. This will be a good thing. For all of us."

She hoped so.

She'd fought against it. Bringing an outsider to their home was tantamount to committing treason from her viewpoint. The Conservancy planned to turn the land adjacent to hers into a park, complete with hiking trails and scenic outlooks. For the last five years, she and other ranchers in the area had leased the land from the federal government. That would stop with his arrival.

She'd known five years ago that she wouldn't be able to lease the land forever. She'd grabbed at the chance then, and so had others like her. Now that land would be taken away and crisscrossed with hiking trails for would-be campers and hikers. Some might call her attitude selfish. She saw it as survival.

The only concession she'd been able to wrangle from her uncle was that the man wouldn't be staying in the house. That smacked of taking on paying guests, an indignity she hadn't been able to deal with.

Pride, her Uncle Charlie had told her often enough, was going to be her downfall.

The surveyor would be staying in the cabin. When the arrangements had been made, she'd been agreeably surprised to find that he approved. ''I like my privacy,'' he'd written back.

She'd drawn her own picture of him from that: a fussy little man with a calculator and notebook. He'd probably have pitted skin and a nervous manner.

Well, she'd promised. And a member of the Two

Feathers family always kept their promises. That was how she thought of herself. Though her last name was legally Roberts, she considered herself one of the People.

Once she made sure Uncle Charlie was settled for the night, she headed to the office at the back of the house. She looked at the account book and bills littering her desk and wondered when she'd become a paper-pusher instead of a rancher. Each year, the ranch required more and more paperwork. The never-ending paperwork was a constant annoyance, taking her away from the work she loved. If she could swing it financially, she'd hire an accountant and let someone else handle it.

Right now, she was putting every cent she could back into the ranch—buying new equipment, improving the bloodline of her stock, even purchasing a computer for her records. Maybe next year, when she'd paid off the hospital bills, she'd be able to afford the new tractor she'd had her eye on. Slowly, she was whittling them down, but she had a long road ahead of her. She rested her elbow on the desk and propped her chin on the heel of her hand.

Hospital and doctor bills from Uncle Charlie's heart attack had multiplied faster than the pair of rabbits she'd had as a child. She'd signed a banknote and plunged the ranch into debt to pay for his stay in the ICU.

And she'd do it again. Having Uncle Charlie well was worth any sacrifice. He was pretty much recovered now, but she still worried, hovering even when she knew he resented it.

She didn't have time for showing some pencil jockey around, she thought wearily. She didn't have time for all that had to be done now. Ranching required constant work—cattle needed to be sheared, winter wheat needed to be planted, and fences needed to be checked, repaired, and checked again.

She pushed the feelings away with a sigh of impatience. Monthly reports were due in a few days' time. She'd accepted the responsibility, and she didn't shirk what she'd promised to do.

Two hours later, she rotated her shoulders in an effort to relieve the tension knotted between them. She slumped back in her chair. With more resignation than enthusiasm, she shoved away the weariness that cloaked her like a wet blanket and concentrated on making out checks. She was tired, she thought. Absently, she rubbed the back of her neck. The pain there was pretty much constant these days, the sort of ache brought on by too much worry and not enough of anything else.

The following morning, she made good on her promise to Uncle Charlie and rode out to the cabin. An outrider's cabin, it had been used only sporadically over the last few years. It had been modernized to the extent of having plumbing and electricity installed, but that was as far as the amenities went.

She inspected the inside and sighed. Well, she'd known it was run-down after years of neglect, but she hadn't expected it to be *this* dilapidated.

Cobwebs clung to the corners, dust coated the few pieces of furniture, and a stale and musty smell clung to the air. Neglect and decay were evident everywhere. The kitchen and bathroom were tiny, but adequate. Or they would be as soon as she gave them a thorough scrubbing.

She unpacked her cleaning supplies and set to work. Four hours later, she stood back and surveyed her efforts. The cabin was still shabby and run-down, but at least it was relatively clean now.

A glance at her watch confirmed what her stomach had told her hours ago. She dug a sandwich from her saddlebag and munched on it while she stocked the shelves with foodstuffs from home. She then made up the narrow bed with clean sheets, topping it with a Native American blanket. The bright colors cheered the otherwise drab room.

Weariness settled over her. She stretched out on the bed. For only a moment, she promised herself, then she'd be on her way. She certainly didn't want to be here when he arrived.

* * *

Burke Kincaid scanned the road for signs to Hallelujah, Wyoming. The road stretched in front of him, an unbroken ribbon of gray that unfurled over the barren landscape. He'd been told that the town was little more than a blip on the map. When he saw the sign: HALLELUJAH–5 MILES, NEXT EXIT, he pressed harder on the accelerator.

Pulling the letter he'd received from his host, he frowned over the directions. Twenty minutes later, he parked his truck in front of a small cabin. He spent long minutes simply absorbing the beauty that surrounded him. He inhaled sharply, savoring the taste of mountain air, untainted by city smells. A breeze ruffled his hair, carrying the scent of pine and fir . . . and freedom.

The fresh air was symbolic, he thought.

The job represented more than a simple survey. It was his first step into forging a new life for himself. A fast-track career had led him to becoming a major player in corporate takeovers. He'd worked for his entire adult life to reach that point, only to find he no longer wanted it.

Along the way, his wants had changed, his needs had changed, *he* had changed. Throwing away the shackles of working only to accumulate more money had freed him in a way he hadn't known possible.

He'd taken early retirement, cashed in his stock options, and plunged into a new job, a new life. Working in the environmental field, he hoped, would relieve the growing sense of discontent he'd been experiencing.

Fortunately, he had the background to get the job. Years before, he'd worked for an environmental group while putting himself through college. He could still talk the talk. And having worked in the corporate world for more than a dozen years gave him the necessary business credentials so many organizations required.

The land drew him; the harsh plains and ragged peaks were far more appealing than the city's skyline. If he had his way, he'd make this his home permanently.

He pulled out his laptop, the only thing of value he'd brought with him. The rest of his gear could wait.

The inside of the cabin was utilitarian, nearly spartan. A minuscule kitchen held the necessities— a hot plate, sink, and pint-sized refrigerator. No surprises there. He saw a door, which he assumed led to a bathroom. Well, he'd been warned that the cabin held only the basics. It was a far cry from the expensively furnished condo he'd called home for more years than he cared to remember.

Not until he turned did he notice the bed tucked into the far corner of the room. Or the sleeping woman on it.

Now *that* was a surprise.

His heart simply stopped.

The lady wasn't the most beautiful woman he'd ever seen. But she was striking, and that was far more appealing than simple beauty. Her looks weren't candy-box pretty. They were too strong, too dynamic for mere prettiness.

''Sleeping Beauty.'' The words slipped from his lips.

Some Native American blood, he decided, would account for the slash of cheekbones and high brow. Hair the color of a sleek black crow was nearly waist length and caught at her neck by a leather thong. Her skin was pale gold. Idly, he wondered what color her eyes were.

He wasn't left to wonder for long when she jerked upright, her eyes widening at the sight of him. They were blue, he noted, bluer than the sky at midday.

He couldn't be sure whether it had been the sound of his voice or some innate sense warning her that she was no longer alone that awoke her. He rushed to put her at ease and stuck out his hand. ''I'm Burke Kincaid.''

"Cheyenne Roberts." Her hand, small but strong, was swallowed by his.

"I'm here from the Conservancy for Parks and Forests." He smiled, but the lady didn't return it. He felt more than heard her quick intake of breath.

"I know." The clipped tone of her voice made him raise his brows. "You're here to turn one of the most beautiful pieces of earth into a playland for litterbug tourists."

So that was it. Well, better to meet the opposition up front. That way, he knew what he was facing. He'd been warned that many of the locals didn't approve of what he'd been sent to do. Opening the land to hikers and campers wasn't popular with a lot of people. But this land deserved a wider audience than the few rugged people who chose to make their living from it.

He hadn't counted on encountering resistance so soon. He started to explain his mission when she pulled the door open and stepped outside.

He followed more slowly, more interested in her reaction to the land than the land itself, beautiful though it was. "You love it," he said, studying her face.

"Yes." Her voice was clipped, short to the point of rudeness.

He rocked back on his heels, thumbs hooked in

his pockets. ''You don't like me.'' He made it a statement. ''I want to know why.''

''I have no reason to dislike you,'' she said carefully.

''Then why do you?''

''People around here don't have much use for bureaucrats who want to take away the open range and turn it into some kind of theme park for bored yuppies. We make our living from the land and don't take kindly to people who want to play at being cowboy for a day.''

He zeroed in on one point. ''You run your stock on an open range?''

''Look around you.'' Impatience shimmered in her voice. ''We're in the middle of a drought. I *have* to use every bit of range available just to keep my stock alive.'' She let her gaze sweep the sun-scorched ground with its almost nonexistent vegetation, mute evidence of the long months without rain.

''How long's it been going on?''

She swiped at her face with her bandanna. ''Four months.''

''It looks bad.''

''What's the matter, Mr. Kincaid? Don't you like the effects of a drought? Or do you believe that the simple Native Americans can do a rain dance and everything will be all right?'' The heat in her voice was more than a match for the heat that blanketed the land.

Burke fought to keep a tight rein on his own temper. The lady was treating him like he was the greenest of greenhorns. Then his sense of humor kicked in, and a reluctant grin played about his lips. Darn, if she hadn't given him what for. He didn't much like what she'd had to say, but he liked how she'd said it. Courage and fire—the lady had both—in spades.

"It's Burke. You've got a chip on your shoulder, Ms. Roberts."

"Make it Cheyenne. And it's no chip. What I've got is—" She broke off and took a deep breath.

"I'm sorry about your problems. But it doesn't change what I have to do."

"Have to or want to?"

"I understand how you feel, but—"

"You have no idea how I feel. How could you? You're barely here fifteen minutes and you think you know how I feel?" The impatience was back—in spades.

Too late, he recognized how pompous his words must have sounded. He was a newcomer here. He knew enough to realize it would take a long time for him to be accepted. If ever.

"I'm sorry. I didn't mean to offend you." He shoved a hand through his hair and decided he'd better get it over with. ''But I'm here to do a job. I'm sorry if it bothers you, but I believe in what I'm doing.''

''So do I.''

He liked that, the straightforward speaking with no pretty words attached. ''You don't back down.'' He leveled a long look at her. ''You have a job to do. So do I.''

She met his gaze unflinchingly. She was facing him down, he thought with reluctant admiration, in a way no one had done for years.

''Have you always been like this?'' he demanded.

''Like what?''

''Blunt. Curt. Unwilling to listen to anyone's point of view but your own.''

''Thanks.'' She made it sound like the greatest of compliments.

The lady was tough. He respected that. He allowed himself a more thorough study of his unwilling hostess. He'd been right the first time. She was striking, even more so now with her eyes shooting sparks at him and her cheeks bright with color.

She was tall, comfortable against his own six-feet-two, and slender. But beneath the willowy build, he sensed strength. Her hands were ringless and practical, the unpolished nails cut short and square.

She fit here. Not just in the way she was

dressed—the leather vest worn over a denim shirt and the jeans faded to near-white. It was in the way she held herself, the way she was at one with her surroundings. Confidence, rather than arrogance, he thought, gave her the air of authority that sat comfortably upon those slim shoulders.

He'd always thought of blue eyes as cool. Hers spit fire. He wondered if they'd soften if he ever managed to get a smile out of her.

She waited as he gave her a thorough scrutiny. ''Like what you see?''

''Yeah,'' he drawled. He liked it very much.

Her scent settled over him like the morning mist and made him want to smile as much as did her blunt speaking. ''I think we're going to get along just fine.''

Chapter Two

Cheyenne wasn't nearly as optimistic.

She let her gaze slide down the length of him.
There wasn't an ounce of extra flesh on him, she
noted. Nor an ounce of softness. He should have
been soft and flabby, not toned and well muscled,
and very nearly beautiful. Only a nose that had obviously been broken saved him from downright per-
fection. Thick blond hair, the color of wheat ready
to be harvested, framed a lean, hard face.

It was a face that radiated too much strength to
be merely handsome, too much grit to peg him as
the nerdy pencil jockey she'd imagined. Dark gray
eyes, resembling thunderclouds heavy with rain,
met her gaze squarely.

24

He had callouses too, she remembered, flexing her fingers slightly, hard ridges across his palms that no pencil pusher should have known how to acquire. The thought gave her pause. No, he wasn't what she expected. Not in the least.

She scowled at the direction her thoughts were taking. Good-looking men weren't on her agenda. Especially one who looked as if he'd just stepped out of the pages of one of the romance novels she kept stashed under her bed.

''You don't look like a bureaucrat,'' she said and then frowned. Uncle Charlie said her tongue had the wings of the eagle when it should move with the slowness of the turtle.

''Let me guess,'' he said. ''You expected a little man in glasses with his head bent over a clipboard and his nose stuck in a book.''

A smile fought its way to life. ''How'd you know?''

''Comes with the territory.'' His smile echoed her own.

The air went very still. She felt a prickling at the nape of her neck. It was as if every sense was attuned to this man. And she'd known him for only a few minutes. Small tremors shimmered down her spine. She shivered slightly, uneasy at her response to him and annoyed that she had one. She'd never experienced a reaction like this to any man—instant awareness and the feeling that she'd stumbled onto something she didn't understand.

He closed the short distance between them, making her more aware of him than ever. Unlike many large men, Burke Kincaid wore his size comfortably, moving with an easy grace as he walked toward her.

She held her ground, tilting her head up in order to meet his gaze. She wasn't accustomed to that. At five-feet-ten, she was as tall as most men, taller than many. Her chin came up in an automatic reaction.

He turned his gaze toward the land and spread his arms wide to encompass it. ''It's beautiful, this land of yours.''

She nodded jerkily.

''I don't plan on changing that.''

She laughed shortly. ''You want to mark trails.'' She all but sneered the words. ''Make them suitable for city folk to traipse around and litter and make campfires that they don't put out and—''

''Whoa. I'll admit they may *traipse*.'' The amusement in his voice set her teeth on edge. ''But who says they're going to litter? Or start forest fires?''

''City folk always litter. First they backpack with a bunch of canned food. Then they don't want to carry the empties back down, so they toss 'em.'' She'd seen it a hundred times, expected to see it at

least a hundred more. And she'd seen the smolder-
ing fires that inexperienced campers doused with a
bit of water and thought they'd smothered. The dev-
astation wrought from a carelessly extinguished fire
took several lifetimes to erase.

''You're too new here to understand.'' She
squinted into the distance, absorbing the land that
was at the heart of the conflict. It was glorious; it
was also harsh and exacting. Too many had paid
the ultimate price to keep it unspoiled.

She raised her chin another notch. ''It's my
ranch. I'll do what I have to to protect it.''

''You're not what I expected.''

For the first time, Cheyenne smiled with her
whole self. ''Same goes.''

Cheyenne pulled back the gingham curtains and
let the morning sun stream into the big, old-
fashioned kitchen. Her fingers lingered on the curtains, remembering when she and her mother had
made them together.

Her own efforts with the sewing machine had
been clumsy and awkward, but Mama had praised
each straight stitch and helped Cheyenne pick out
the not-so-straight ones. The once-bright red and
white checks had faded until the colors now blurred
together. She ought to replace them. Somehow,
though, she never got around to it.

She wrapped her hands around a cup of tea, warming them. Even though temperatures in the desert could top a hundred degrees during the day, early mornings were chilly.

She pushed open the screen door and wandered out to the back porch. Dawn had just announced itself with an array of colors that defied words. Sunrises in the city couldn't touch those that the country produced. She lifted her face to the sun. Its rays only hinted at the heat that would soon blanket the land. For now, it warmed her and cast a pleasant glow over the outbuildings.

After gulping down the breakfast of oatmeal and juice Uncle Charlie had insisted she eat, she headed to the barn. A ride would smooth away the rough edges of a nearly sleepless night. The soft whickerings and pungent smell of horses soothed her as nothing else could.

''Hey there, girl,'' she said, holding out a carrot for Taffy.

Taffy whinnied in pleasure at the unexpected treat. Cheyenne watched as the horse chomped down the carrot in one bite.

''You feeling frisky this morning?'' she asked, sidestepping as Taffy nuzzled her for another carrot. ''Up for a ride?''

Another whinny answered in the affirmative.

Pink fingers of light poked their way through the

sky, a promise of the day to come. Clouds scuttled across the morning gray. She was due to show Kincaid around today, but she had an hour to herself.

The early morning hours were precious, a time when she could meditate and reflect. Her Shoshone heritage had given her an appreciation for the quiet art of introspection.

Cheyenne took the ride from the valley up to the foothills ringing her land at an easy pace. The sheep were fat and sassy, she noted with satisfaction. A few more weeks and it'd be time for shearing.

No doubt about it, the ranch was prospering. Slowly, to be sure, but the signs were there. Fences were in good condition. Cash crops and raising sheep in the pastures not fit for cattle had buffered Sweet Water Ranch against the fluctuating market for beef.

She'd also experimented with wind-generated power. Her neighbors had had a good laugh at her expense when she built a series of windmills along the southern boundary of her property. The last laugh was hers a year ago, though, when her windmills kept the power going on the Sweet Water when a snowstorm took down the electrical lines throughout the county. Someday, she wanted to install a backup generator for the main house and outbuildings.

Yeah, right, she thought. Like she had any extra

cash. Money was in short supply, and it didn't look like things were going to change anytime soon. Not with Uncle Charlie's hospital bills still to pay.

After his heart attack, Uncle Charlie had slumped into a depression. He never complained, never grumbled at what fate had dealt him. But the life had gone out of his eyes. And the joy.

She'd hired extra help and spent the hours sitting with him at the hospital, talking, cajoling, and bullying him into getting better. She begged the doctor to release Uncle Charlie early and promised that she'd keep him quiet, if only she could bring him home.

Some said she ought to have put her uncle in a nursing home. The idea abhorred her. She'd hired a private nurse to spell her when she couldn't be with him and had done the rehab exercises with him herself. She'd kept his mind interested even when his body couldn't respond. She'd done what she had to. She hadn't thought about it; she'd simply done it. A person didn't look for praise for doing what had to be done.

It wasn't simply a question of honor that Charlie remain at home. It was a matter of family. And Uncle Charlie was family.

The screech of a hawk made her look up. The sight of the bird gliding through the cloud-heavy sky transfixed her. She watched as it swooped to pounce upon a prairie dog, then soar upward once more, the prey caught in its talons.

Some might be repelled by the scene. She knew better, understanding it was but one part of nature's cycle. Each part had its place, a piece of the whole.

City folk didn't understand. Unbidden, a picture of Burke formed in her mind. Would he? she wondered. Would he understand that nature wasn't always pretty or tidy? That it couldn't always be wrapped up in facts and figures? She was surprised—and dismayed—to find that the answer mattered.

When she discovered the cabin empty, she went looking for him. *Darn.* She didn't have time to go looking for some greenhorn. She found him at a dried-up riverbed, field glasses hanging around his neck and a spotting scope in his hand.

He was overwhelmingly handsome, standing there against the backdrop of mountain and sky. A fawn-colored shirt and faded jeans showed off his rangy build to advantage. The morning sun glinted off his hair, untidy as though he'd shoved his hand through it. Dimples dented his cheeks, and his eyes squinted against the glare of the sun. No woman alive, she thought, could resist the picture he made.

No woman, she amended, except her.

She was immune to gorgeous males with hair like golden wheat and eyes that could melt a woman's bones at one hundred paces. But that didn't mean she couldn't look . . . and appreciate.

He must have sensed her presence for he looked up then and grinned. "Hey, pretty lady."

That earned a scowl from her. She cocked her head to one side. "You lost, city boy? We were supposed to meet back at the cabin."

"Sorry. I was just admiring the view."

Her lips softened into a smile. She understood the awe that the land could instill in someone. Its beauty still drew her, and she'd spent her life here.

He was beginning to understand her attitude toward keeping things as they were. It didn't change what he had to do, but he softened his tone and reached out a hand. "Listen, Cheyenne—"

"You got something to say, city boy?"

With an effort, he held onto his temper. The lady was going to call him that one time too often. Until then, he'd bide his time.

"No, ma'am. You?"

She spread her arm to indicate the vastness before them. "It's my land." She said it with such simple arrogance that he was tempted to laugh. He caught it in time.

"You're right. So why don't you show me around? We'll get to the *government's* land soon enough." He emphasized the word only slightly.

She didn't want to. He understood that. But she'd

given her word, and she'd keep it or die trying. He understood that as well, and respected it.

''What do you want to know?'' she asked.

How long it's going to take me to knock down those walls around you, he thought. ''Everything you can show me.''

''You got it.'' She paused, a wisp of a smile touching her lips. ''City boy.''

But it wasn't said with malice this time, and he smiled as well. ''Thanks.''

The first stop was her ranch where she picked out a mount for him. Traveler, a three-year-old gelding, stood sixteen hands high easily. A big roan, he danced about in his stall, clearly eager to be out.

''You trying to kill me off?'' Burke asked, keeping a healthy distance from the stall.

''I'm giving you the best gelding we have. Or would you like Jenny?'' She gestured to the next stall where a docile little mare resided, her dainty head tilted inquiringly. She was ten years old and as gentle as one of the lambs.

Burke grimaced. ''Traveler it is.''

''He's just showing off,'' Cheyenne said and opened the stall door to lead the horse out.

Outside, Traveler pranced around, showing off like a rambunctious child. She leaned over to swat the big horse on the nose. ''No more of that, or you won't get your treat.''

Traveler nuzzled her cheek. "See?" she demanded of Burke. "He's just a big baby." She handed the gelding a stick of licorice, which he gobbled down with a chomp of his huge teeth.

Cheyenne let Burke saddle Traveler, snickering as he fumbled the job. The man may have looked like a Greek god, but he was all thumbs when it came to horses. Her conscience pricked her. Traveler wasn't a horse for novices. She was about to say so, to offer him Taffy, when Burke gathered the reins in a practiced manner and mounted. The bungling greenhorn had vanished; in his place was an experienced horseman.

She'd been had. Big time. The man handled Traveler like a pro.

"You like making a fool out me?" She all but snarled the words.

"No. Just living up—or down—to your expectations."

She supposed she deserved that. "You're right." She stuck out her hand, pleased when he took it. "I'm not normally such a jerk."

"I didn't think you were."

A truce had been declared.

Burke put Traveler through his paces around the corral. His movements were quintessentially male, economical and sure, drawing her attention to his hands. They were large, like the man himself, but oddly graceful. And competent. She wondered what it would feel like to have them stroke her hair. Or her cheek.

''Where'd you learn to handle a horse like that?'' she asked when he turned Traveler back to where she stood.

''I spent summers with my grandpa. He owned a ranch in southern Colorado. We were riding before we walked.''

''We?''

''My sister and I. Carla was a couple of years younger, but she was always determined to do anything I did. When I told her she was too little to sit a horse, she hauled off and punched me in the face.'' He traced the crooked line of his nose ruefully. ''Broke my nose.''

Cheyenne laughed delightedly. ''Your sister broke your nose? I love it.''

His grin was wry. ''After all the bleeding stopped, that was her reaction.''

They kept an easy pace, content with the day and each other.

''Why are you helping me?'' he asked after a long stretch of silence. ''You made it pretty plain how you feel.''

''I gave my word,'' she said simply. There were

few enough things in the world that a person could count on. She liked to think her word was one of them.

"That's it?"

"That's it."

She pushed them both, wanting to show him what made this land so special. They kept their lunch break brief, not wanting to waste a moment. To her surprise, she discovered she was hungry, the fresh air sharpening her appetite.

Burke put down the thick slabs of roast beef on Uncle Charlie's homemade bread and the applesauce cake with equal relish. "You keep feeding me like this, and I'll have to get me some new jeans," he said.

Not much chance of that, she thought, looking at his flat stomach and narrow hips in admiration.

"I thought we'd declared a truce," he said by the end of the day, pushing back his hat. Sweat clung to his forehead, darkening his thick blond hair.

She glanced at him, not surprised when he looked as if he could ride for another six hours. Her own legs ached from hugging Taffy's side. Burke Kincaid was more than she'd expected, on every level.

"I thought you wanted to get a feel for the land."

"I did," he said ruefully. "I just didn't plan on doing it all in one day."

"You know what they say. Be careful what you

wish for—you may get it.'' She dismounted and left Taffy untethered. She was a good enough mount not to wander far.

Burke followed suit. By unspoken consent, they started walking. He carried himself well, she noted, his long legs eating up the distance with an ease she could only envy. He wore the Western-style jeans and boots like a man accustomed to them.

A large root caught the toe of her boot, and she felt herself falling. She landed hard, the breath knocked from her. Annoyed with herself, she started to push herself up when a large hand closed around hers and pulled.

A greenhorn mistake, she thought with a spurt of self-disgust. If she hadn't been so preoccupied studying the man, she'd have sidestepped the root.

''Thanks.''

They spent the rest of the day in the high country. Part of his job was to make a count of the deer, elk, and moose in the area. Cheyenne took him to a ridge overlooking a stream-fed meadow where the animals gathered.

A bull elk was the first to appear.

''Magnificent,'' Burke breathed.

''Wapiti.'' She felt his gaze on her. ''Shawnee for elk.''

''Wapiti.'' He said the word as though testing it, tasting it.

She liked the sound of it on his tongue and felt a stirring within her. The sight of the huge animal was awesome. But it was more than that. It was the way Burke looked, as if he'd found something precious and rare. He cared. The thought gave her hope. If she could convince him that the land deserved something better than to become the playland of uneducated tourists, maybe she could keep things the way they were.

She recognized her plan as impractical, even foolish. Burke had a job to do. But so did she. Her job was to save the open range. Her motives weren't altruistic. It was a matter of survival. She knew the importance of educating others about the land and the animals who made their homes there. She also knew that same land could be destroyed if it wasn't protected.

Burke wondered what was going through Cheyenne's mind. The woman was an enigma: cool and aloof one moment, warm and friendly the next, angry and disapproving after that.

He reached for her hand, wanting to share this moment. The elk, at least six hundred pounds, was as proud and arrogant as the mountains where he made his home. Burke let out a long breath he hadn't known he was holding. The picture before him would be forever imprinted on his mind.

"Thank you," he said quietly. "Thank you for bringing me here."

He turned her hand over. Her nails were short and unpolished, her skin red and work-roughened. "I've always thought you can tell a lot about people by their hands."

"What are you? A palm reader?"

"Uh-uh. A man who knows hard work when he sees it." He stroked the faint ridges of callouses along her palms. "And feels it."

"Ranching doesn't leave much time for manicures." She eased her hand from his.

He saw her flush and guessed at its cause. "Don't be embarrassed. Your hands tell me you care about what you do."

They rode back to the cabin in silence, a comfortable, friendly silence, suited to two people who were in accord with each other and their surroundings. Beneath Cheyenne's fatigue, though, was a growing sense of excitement. She'd start putting her plan into action tomorrow.

She spent the next few days showing Burke the special places: the glen where cautious does brought their fawns, the hot springs that bubbled sulphurous waters even in the worst of droughts, and the sheer cliffs where the golden eagles made their home.

By the end of the week, Burke seemed as enchanted with the land as she was. "This land of yours is the most beautiful I've ever come across."

Pride welled within her, And hope underscored her words. "You understand."

"I understand that it deserves to be appreciated by everyone, not just the few people fortunate enough to live here." His voice rose in enthusiasm. "Can't you see it? Hundreds, thousands of people, every month, coming here to fall in love with this piece of earth. Just like I have."

She could see it all right—the land rutted with the tracks of four-wheel drives and motorcycles, the litter that backpackers left behind, the charred remains of a forest fire—she could see it all too well.

"You're painting the worst-case scenario," he said as she put her feelings into words.

"I'm not painting anything. I'm telling you what's happened in the past, what will happen again."

"What's the matter?" he asked. "Are you so scared of the idea of sharing your little world that you're threatened at the very idea of letting others see it?"

It was more important than ever that he understood how much this meant to her. If he could accept that, then maybe . . . She gave him a long look. He *did* understand. She'd seen the quick flare of empathy in his eyes when she'd told him of the drought.

She pointed to the horizon, a strip of purple that banded the prairie. ''See that?''

He let his gaze follow in the direction she pointed.

''The land,'' she said impatiently. ''The land. It's what this is all about. The land is a living thing. It's what makes us what we are.''

''We?''

''The people who make their living from the land,'' she said impatiently, knowing he was listening and afraid she might never get another chance. She faced him squarely, putting every bit of persuasion she could muster into her voice. ''And that means just about everyone around here—the people who sell to the ranchers, the people who grind the wheat, the people at the meat packers—the land's a part of us. When something threatens it, we fight back. We have to.''

Instant defense for what he was doing sprang to his lips. But his voice was mild when he said, ''You can't fight progress.''

''I don't see it as progress.''

The impatience had left her voice. It was quiet now, quiet and controlled. But something else lay just beneath. He tried to pinpoint what it was. Desperation. Fear.

She wouldn't admit to it, he realized. A woman like Cheyenne wouldn't like acknowledging anything akin to weakness. Even without knowing her very well, he sensed that. She was as proud and unyielding as the land she was so fiercely protective of. She was as much a part of the land as it was of her. Her lips had flattened to a hard line and her eyes shuttered against giving anything more away.

He'd learned to recognize that look even in the short time he'd known her, the look that told him to back off. Something had hurt her at one time, something that had nothing to do with the land. Something or someone? The question intrigued him, and for a moment he forgot they were on opposite sides.

''Is it wrong to want to defend what's mine?'' she asked.

''No. But that . . .'' He pointed to the land to the east of hers, the land he was sent to survey . . . ''isn't yours.''

''No, it isn't.''

The hitch in her voice tugged at his heart. It was immediate and overwhelming.

He was trained in facts, what he could observe and measure with his own eyes. The effect Cheyenne had on him wasn't logical, wasn't reasonable, wasn't sensible. But it was there.

"I know my job's not going to win me any pop-ularity contests," he said.

"But you intend to go ahead."

He nodded. "I have to."

He curved his knuckles under her chin, lifting her head just enough so that her gaze was on a level with his own. "You thought if you showed me around, showed me what the land meant to you and the other ranchers, I'd change my mind. Tell my boss it won't work."

She shook off his hand. "Something like that."

"I'm sorry. I can't do it. If there was another way, I'd jump at it. But there isn't."

The quiet sincerity in his voice convinced her he was telling the truth. But it didn't change what was between them. She looked at their linked hands. Each was strong yet different. . . . As different as the two of them were. Yet they fit together.

At some point, their hands fell apart. A symbol, Cheyenne wondered, of the differences that divided them? That would always divide them?

She looked at him for a long moment. "I suppose you would." Was that regret she saw in his eyes? Maybe there was still a chance. . . .

"I have to do what I think is right."

Her hopes died at his words. "So do I."

Battle lines had been drawn. The truce was over.

Chapter Three

Cheyenne remained where she was for long moments. Some of the day's brightness dimmed though the sun continued to beat down on her. Reluctant admiration built in her as she watched Burke ride off. The man had a lot going for him, including the easy way he sat a horse. For a moment, she knew a pang of regret. Burke Kincaid was someone she could like, but she feared their loyalties would always divide them.

She was uncomfortable with the thought that she'd been in the wrong. It wasn't a position she was accustomed to occupying, and it left her with a bad taste in her mouth. She owed him an apology.

Burke had a right to do his job. If the circumstances had been different, she'd probably be offering to help him with real enthusiasm. But, darn it, the circumstances weren't different.

The land was her heritage, her link to the past, and her passport to the future. She had plowed whatever extra money she had—and there was precious little—back into the land. There was too little money and too little time: a rancher's lament.

Cheyenne slammed a fist in her palm. He'd been disappointed in her. It had been in his eyes just before he'd taken off. And it mattered, she discovered, mattered too much, what he thought of her, what he felt for her, how he looked at her.

He mattered too much. It was a sobering realization, one she wasn't comfortable admitting. But it was there.

The late-afternoon heat beat down on her. Her clothes were covered with brown dust by the time she reached the house; her throat was so dry that she could barely swallow; and her spirits were lower than the underside of a lizard's belly.

She spent the rest of the day stewing in her own guilt. When Uncle Charlie found her, she was no closer to absolving herself than she had been hours ago.

"What is it that troubles you?" he asked.

''Nothing.''

His eyes reproved her. ''You will tell me when the time is right.''

She didn't know whether to be annoyed or amused at his assumption that she was keeping something from him. The fact was, she was. But she couldn't confide to her uncle that a man she'd met only days ago had her twisted in knots.

''When you find your tongue, come to me. My body is feeble, but my eyes can still see a troubled heart.''

His reference to his feeble body wasn't lost on her. She knew he resented her insistence that he remain inside. She didn't need to look at Uncle Charlie to know where the sun had etched fine lines around his eyes and mouth. But they were only outward signs of the age that was slowly but surely claiming him. His hair, once as dark as her own, was now silver. He still wore it in the long braids that hung down his back.

She pushed away the memories of him weak and broken in a hospital bed, memories that still had the power to send chills skating down her spine even after all these months. He was well now, and she'd do everything in her power to keep him that way. Even if it meant keeping him away from the land he loved.

When she was ready to talk, Uncle Charlie was

there. The story came out in bits and pieces. "I tried to persuade him to abandon his job," she finished. It shamed her to admit it.

There were no words of reproach. Only a quiet squeezing of her hand. "You will find a way to make it right," Uncle Charlie said.

In her office an hour later, Cheyenne drummed her fingers on her desk, the report awaiting her attention untouched.

Darn. She had a feeling she could like Burke under other circumstances. She shook her head and sighed in regret. Fate had put them on opposite sides of the fence. Granted, the man got under her skin, but that didn't give her the right to try to use him as she had. Crow was a bitter dish to swallow. And admitting that she'd been wrong was the bitterest of all.

Her thoughts churned around and around until she could stand it no longer. She slipped on a jacket and let herself outside.

A velvety darkness closed around her; a breeze feathered over her face. The weeks she'd spent in the city when Uncle Charlie had been hospitalized had convinced her she'd never be happy away from the land. In the city the stars were frequently lost in the glitter of the lights. Here the night was thick and black, emphasizing the brilliance of the stars. Nothing interfered with nature's splendor.

Then, too, there were the sounds. The chirping of crickets, the scuttling of a small animal, and the slithering of a snake or lizard over the ground created a harmony that rivaled that of renowned symphonies.

She remembered the noises that had routinely bombarded her ears during her stay in the city. Horns blasting, sirens screaming, and engines roaring were a poor substitute for the music that serenaded her now.

Reluctantly, she headed back to the house. She had a heavy day planned for tomorrow, and she had a feeling she was going to need every bit of courage and nerve she had—and then some.

Morning light came early, she thought as she rubbed her eyes. A glance at her clock told her it was only 5:30, but the rosy light of dawn was already pushing away the last of the night's darkness.

Her muscles protested as she climbed out of bed. She'd expected to fall asleep immediately the night before, but the events of the day had replayed through her mind with the precision of a video recording. She shook off the doubts that had pestered her during the night and grinned as she remembered her uncle's words: ''Crow is sweetened when the words are sincere.''

''You were right, Uncle,'' she whispered.

An early morning chill penetrated her thin cotton blouse. She pulled on her jacket and turned up the collar. She knew that the temperature would soar soon enough, though, as the sun climbed higher into the sky.

She headed to the barn and saddled Taffy.

When she didn't find Burke at the cabin, she started toward the ridge where they'd spotted the elk a few days ago.

Did he appreciate the beauty of the land? Or was it just one big wilderness to him, the town quaint, the people quainter? The idea twisted in her gut. She clamped down on the direction her reflections had taken.

Irritated, she took off her hat, wiped the sweat from her forehead, and then jammed the hat back on her head before nudging Taffy on. Elk had knocked over the fence bordering the north pasture—again. If she didn't get it repaired soon, the cattle would find it and wander away. Dumb animals didn't know enough to stay where it was safe.

She lifted her head to stare at the wide expanse of prairie, as words from the past echoed through her mind. ''Take care of Mother Earth and she will return it one hundredfold,'' her uncle had said many times. Cheyenne had listened.

The sun beat down with merciless intensity, burning away any trace of the earlier chill. She pushed her hat back and let the slight breeze cool her fore-head. Untying the kerchief from around her neck, she wiped the perspiration from her face and thought ruefully of the full canteen she'd left sitting on the kitchen table. Only a tenderfoot went off without a canteen.

The nickname brought a smile to her lips. Her uncle had called her that the first summer he'd come to live with them. It had been a source of pride that he hadn't had cause to apply it to her again. That she'd forgotten hers today was mute evidence of her state of mind. Well, she'd make her apologies and get on with the job she'd promised to do.

Burke held out a map, frowned over it, and then stuffed it back into his shirt pocket. He'd studied maps of the area and zeroed in on the canyon just west of Sweet Water Ranch as a likely spot for the herd to graze.

He didn't push Traveler. The gelding seemed to sense his mood and kept the pace easy. Burke wanted to take his time and *feel* the land, a land as wild and free and unclaimed as it must have been two hundred years ago. A dry wind whipped across his face, stinging his eyes with sand. He brushed it away and then licked his lips.

An hour later, he was watching for any sign of the deer and elk. Never one of his strengths, his

After a few minutes, she pulled out the thermometer and checked the reading. So far, it was normal.

The cow gave a weak bawl of pain.

''It's all right,'' she murmured, whether to Sheba or herself, she wasn't sure.

Cheyenne guided a tiny hoof out of the birth canal. It was quickly followed by another. ''Just a little bit more,'' she coaxed. ''We're almost there.''

A final whimper caused her to wince in sympathy for Sheba. ''There's another one,'' she said, her voice rising in excitement. ''Two calves. ''C'mon, Sheba. You can do it. Don't give up now.''

Burke crouched closer, fascinated by Cheyenne's competence as well as by the delivery itself. He'd done his own share of delivering calves and foals on his grandfather's ranch. But that had been years ago. The wonder he'd felt then came rushing back.

She spared him a quick smile before resuming delivering Sheba's second baby.

''Burke, look,'' she cried when the second baby appeared. ''Aren't they beautiful?''

''Beautiful,'' he said, his gaze still on Cheyenne. Her arms and clothes were coated with blood and birth fluids, but it was her eyes that held his attention. They shone with an inner light that mocked even the brilliance of the sun that beat down on the roof of the shed. ''Beautiful,'' he repeated, his voice hoarse with emotion.

"Help me pat them down," she said and began gently rubbing the tiny animals with straw.

He imitated her actions, gingerly patting the calves.

"Look, Sheba. You have two babies." Cheyenne gently pushed the little animals forward.

Something warm wrapped itself around his heart.

"Uncle Charlie," she said. "I need you to fix up some of your gruel for Sheba."

He started out.

"You worry about him," Burke said, watching her follow the old man's progress toward the house.

"He had a heart attack six months ago. The doctors said he might never recover. He proved them wrong."

Love, he thought. It was pure and simple and overwhelming love he heard in her voice. It tugged at him.

The lady continued to surprise him. She was tough when she needed to be and fiercely loyal to those she loved. The contrasts, strength tempered by gentleness, appealed to him as much as did her striking face and first-class pair of legs.

"He looks like he'd be pretty handy with the animals."

"He is. Was." There was a crispness to her voice. "Ever since his attack, he's been working inside."

''Has he been with you long?''

Her smile was wide as the Western sky. ''He helped raise me.''

''You love him very much.''

''He's family.''

Family, he thought. It didn't have to be traditional to be full of love. And this one had it.

''What about your parents?''

''My parents split up when I was five.'' She shrugged. ''No big deal.''

But it was, he thought. Unless he missed his guess, it was a very big deal.

''What happened?''

''My father took off. We never heard from him again.'' The subject was clearly closed. All right, he thought. Her father was off-limits. She was still hurting over it, even if she didn't realize it.

''How's Uncle Charlie taking it, having to stay inside?''

A shadow of pain sliced across her face. ''He tolerates it.''

''Tolerates? That sounds pretty lukewarm.''

It did to her too.

''Why does he do it? He looks pretty fit to me.'' In fact, the old man looked darn good with an energy Burke could only envy.

''For me.'' The shadow had deepened. ''He does

it for me. He knows I couldn't bear it if something happened to him.''

''So you keep him locked up inside?''

''It's not like that.'' Defensiveness had crept into her voice.

''Isn't it?''

''No.''

He let it go. For now.

She'd intrigued him. Her obvious love for the land was something he could understand and respect. Her love for her great-uncle was yet another facet of a woman he was increasingly attracted to. He liked the lady. She fought for what she believed in. Not many men would have stood up to him the way she had. But she was also totally a woman. She had that rare combination of guts and femininity.

''What do you want from me?'' she asked.

Everything. The admission took his breath away. He inhaled deeply and reminded himself to sound calm and rational. ''Friendship. And maybe a little cooperation.''

That won a smile from her, and his spirits soared.

''I've been wanting to do this since the first time I set eyes on you.''

He bent his head and took her lips with his own.

Chapter Four

The kiss was like nothing she'd ever experienced. Had her heart ever beat so fast, her body ever felt so alive? She didn't think so.

His mouth hovered over hers, a brush of lips, no more. Then he deepened the kiss, his hand cradling the nape of her neck. His touch was as gentle as a summer breeze, but there was strength as well.

Her arms found their way around his neck. The reaction was as natural as breathing in and breathing out. She pressed closer to him, needing the contact, the warmth. He smelled of soap and the scent that was uniquely his. He drew her closer until she could scarcely breathe. When she realized what was happening, what she was feeling, she pulled back.

"This could become a habit," he said, tracing the line of her lower lip with a gentle finger, the caress as soft as a whisper.

His words had her cheeks heating with color. A tiny pulse throbbed at the base of her throat.

He settled his hands on her shoulders, the gesture at once protective and possessive.

She pushed her hair back from her face. "You shouldn't have done that."

"Why?"

His breath tickled her neck. When his hands moved lower to caress her arms, a tremor shivered through her. She worked to level her breathing.

"Because . . ." *Because I don't understand what's happening!* she wanted to shout. *Because I don't want it to happen.* But she couldn't say any of that, and so she remained silent. Old defenses shifted into place, accompanied by a familiar tensing of her lips.

"Why?" he repeated gently.

She settled for a part of the truth. "We scarcely know each other."

"I wouldn't say that." He skimmed a finger down her cheek. "I know you love the land. And your uncle. I know you fight for what you believe." And across her lips. "Seems like I know the important things."

Her eyes beseeched him to understand, though her lips remained silent.

''There'll be another time,'' he promised.

Another time. What was she supposed to make of that? she wondered. She didn't want there to be another time. The honest part of her called her a liar. She wanted it. She wanted it too much.

Despite her resolve, Burke kept creeping into her thoughts. Why did she find herself thinking of him at odd moments? It didn't matter what she was doing—putting up fence, tending a sick lamb, or working on the end-of-the month reports, her mind conjured up pictures of him. The man had invaded her thoughts to the point that she found herself doodling his name in the margins of the paper.

The acknowledgment had her lips tightening in annoyance. There was something about him.... Something that defied the ruthless logic she applied to the rest of her life . . . something that she was powerless to resist.

She pushed the thought away, angry that she'd entertained it even for a moment. Another loss like the one she'd experienced last week and she'd be in serious trouble. Given the uncertain price of wool, the losses due to the drought, and the constant need for repairs to equipment that should have been

retired years ago, the profit margin in sheep ranching was minimal even in good years. Add to that
the loss of ten of her sheep, and she was looking at
some hard times. Hank and Quinn had caught the
marauding wolves, but that didn't mean it wouldn't
happen again.

Ever since she'd graduated from college, she'd
worked to build the ranch. It'd taken every bit of
energy and every cent she had . . . plus some she
hadn't.

Then Uncle Charlie had taken sick. He'd waved
off the first sign of weakness, a shortness of breath.
Uneasily, she'd accepted his explanation that he'd
overworked. When he complained of a pain in his
arm, she didn't wait. She'd ignored his objections
and called an ambulance. A fist of fear had knotted
in her chest when he'd collapsed and the diagnosis
was massive pulmonary damage.

The memory of Burke's kiss managed to intrude
upon her mind for the rest of the day. It was there
when she helped Hank and Quinn string fence. It
was there when she checked on Sheba. It was even
there when she stole a few moments to herself at
the end of the day to read a chapter in the romance
she kept tucked beneath her bed.

When she realized that she was superimposing
Burke's image on the hero's face on the book's

cover, she threw the book down and determined to go to sleep. But his face intruded upon her dreams and she awoke restless and annoyed.

She hadn't slept worth a darn, thanks to a certain blond-haired man and a kiss that should never have happened. Bleary-eyed, she stumbled into the bathroom and stared at her reflection. Aside from the residue of confusion in her eyes, she looked very close to normal. She felt as though she'd been caught in a tornado, tossed about and battered, adrift in a world turned suddenly upside down.

But there was nothing to indicate that less than a day ago she'd been treated to the most searing kiss she'd ever experienced. There was nothing to hint that her emotions were churning in a never-ceasing tumult, nothing to suggest that she had turned a corner she hadn't even known she was approaching.

She spent a longer than usual time in the shower, trying to scrub away the memory of the kiss. But it stubbornly clung, until she finally gave up the unproductive activity.

She dressed hurriedly and headed to the barn. The familiar smells and noises of the horses were reassuring. Burke was invading her thoughts, her dreams, her very soul. And she wasn't going to put up with it.

With that resolved, she was able to settle down to work. She started cleaning the tack that hung in the corner of the barn. She gave herself up to the task she'd performed hundreds of times before. The work was steady, nearly monotonous; it soothed her by its very repetition. She knew herself well enough to understand that this sort of mood overtook her when she was having difficulty blocking out something that worried her.

Something. Or some*one*.

When Uncle Charlie came to find her, she'd finished. A pleasant sense of accomplishment went a long way to banishing troublesome thoughts.

He made a long study of her face. ''You are troubled, Daughter.''

''No.'' But her voice was faint and lacked confidence.

''When it is time, you will tell me what causes you such anguish.''

The answer sprang to her lips, but she kept it to herself: a man with gray eyes that could darken to the color of storm clouds when he bent to kiss her. Uncle Charlie would tell her that the spirits had sent Burke Kincaid to her. She wasn't ready to hear that.

''I'm fine,'' she said shortly.

She was grateful when he didn't pursue the subject. She knew him well enough to recognize that Uncle Charlie would hold his peace until he felt she was ready to talk. He had an uncanny sense of timing that she had cause over and over again to appreciate.

"Steady," she crooned to the big gray gelding.

It was a new venture for her, boarding and training horses for other ranchers and city folk who didn't have the time or patience to do it themselves. Silverado was the first in what she hoped would be a long line of Sweet Water–trained mounts.

To her pleasure, Silverado didn't back off but stood still while she ran her hand across his back.

"See? It's not so bad. Pretty soon you might even like it."

He pranced away, his head high.

"Show-off," she said, smiling fondly at him.

Cautiously, he approached her, waiting for the treat she always kept in her pocket. She pulled out a stick of licorice and let him take it from her hand.

"Good boy." She chanced another pat on his neck. Satisfied with the day's work, she backed off. She could undo all her progress by pushing too hard, too fast. In the last few weeks, she'd managed to get him to accept a bridle. It wasn't much, but it represented progress. She held on to that.

A sand lizard slithered across the ground.

Silverado reared back, his hooves slicing through the air. She backed away slowly. She wouldn't stand a chance if the horse decided to strike out at her. A moment was all it would take for her to be badly injured. Or worse.

Her shoulder still bore the scar where a spooked mare's razor-sharp hooves had caught her before she had managed to roll out of the way. Pictures of what the gelding could do to her filled her mind, each more horrifying than the last.

She sidestepped just in time to avoid the lethal hooves. ''Easy,'' she soothed. ''That's right. No one's going to hurt you.''

Silverado gave a sharp whinny but settled down. She chanced a pat to his neck, relieved when he didn't back away. Slowly, they were forging a bond. If there was trust, then the rest would come.

She heard a sharp whoosh of relief. For a second, she thought it was her own before realizing it had come from behind her. She whirled around.

''What do you think you're doing?'' Burke walked toward her, hands fisted on his hips. He was panting heavily, chest heaving.

She let out a shaky breath, her reaction only now setting in. ''What does it look like?''

''You could've been killed.''

''Nothing happened.''

''*This* time.'' He closed the remaining distance between them and placed his hands on her shoulders, as though to make sure she was really all right. His gaze searched her face. He fit a finger under her chin and studied her face. What he saw there must have satisfied him, for he gave an almost imperceptible nod.

She couldn't help the small tremor that shuddered through her. He drew her close and wrapped his arms around her.

Silverado had calmed down now, the stench of his fear tapering off in the fresh air.

Burke kept her close. ''You shouldn't be working with him alone.''

He continued to hold her, and she wasn't inclined to put an end to it. At least not yet. There was something solid about him that made her feel safe. It pleased her. It also scared her.

''I have a job to do.''

''Get someone to help you.'' The words came out as an order, stiffening her spine.

It was time to end the embrace. She withdrew from his arms, surprised at how much she already missed their warmth. ''Burke, I've been working with stock since I was old enough to sit a horse. I don't take unnecessary risks.''

''What do you call what you just did?''

She poked a finger at his chest. ''I was brought up on this land. I've seen what can happen to someone who gets trampled. It's not pretty. I'm not fool enough to let that happen.'' Annoyance sharpened her voice.

''I never said you were a fool. But when people are totally involved in what they're doing, they may take chances they wouldn't ordinarily take.''

She threw back her head, drawing his attention to the slim column of her throat. ''I've been taking care of myself for a long time. I don't need some bureaucrat from the city telling me how to handle my stock.''

''It sure looked like it.'' Sarcasm dripped from each word.

Cheyenne was about to tell him once more that she could take care of herself when she realized it was concern, not anger, that had darkened his eyes to a stormy gray.

''I'm all right,'' she said quietly. A stab of shame pierced her anger. He was right. She *had* been caught up in her work, not paying sufficient attention to her surroundings. If she had, she might have seen the lizard and guessed at its effect on Silverado.

''You're right,'' she said at last. ''I should have been paying more attention.''

He drew her to him once more. ''I just don't want anything happening to you.''

Confused, and not a little dismayed, by the pleasure his words gave her, she tried to pull away. But he wasn't having any of it. "I didn't know you cared," she said, in what was supposed to be a flippant tone. Instead, her voice had turned unaccountably husky.

His lips quirked into a faint smile. "Let's just say you've grown on me."

He gave her a quick kiss, the kind that shouldn't have left her breathless or staring after him even when he'd walked away.

But it did.

Burke stared at the screen of his laptop, but it was Cheyenne's face he saw. A frown blunted his brow as he recalled how close she'd come to being trampled. Somewhere he'd read the phrase "blood running cold" and had discounted it as some writer's purple prose. At that moment, he'd understood it.

A wry smile tugged at his lips. Cheyenne didn't pull her punches. She'd told him what was what in no uncertain terms. That was one of the things he liked best about her. She wasn't afraid to say what she meant. His smile died. He didn't want her hurt. She'd become special to him.

He stood. He owed her an apology, and he wasn't going to get any work done until he'd made it. He saddled Traveler and headed to Cheyenne's place.

If he was lucky, he'd find her at home. If not, well, he wouldn't mind a ride on the prairie today. Convincing her to accept his apology was another matter.

He found her in the barn, using a pitchfork. Without a word, he picked up another and began mucking out the stalls with her. They worked in companionable silence.

"Did you want something?" she asked after a while.

"I wanted to apologize. I acted like some kind of two-bit bureaucrat, giving out orders without thinking them through. Sorry."

She extended her hand. "Apology accepted. If you can wait, I'll be finished here in a little while." She turned her attention back to the mucking out, her lower lip caught between her teeth as she concentrated on her task.

He smiled as he watched her. She wasn't afraid of getting her hands dirty. He liked that about her. In fact, there were a lot of things to like about Cheyenne Roberts.

A wisp of dark hair fell across her face, and she pushed it back, giving him a clear view of her profile. Her cheeks were flushed with exertion, the heady color making her more beautiful than ever.

She spared him a smile before returning to the job at hand. By the time they were finished, he was adding another piece to the whole that made up Cheyenne. She wasn't afraid of hard work or of getting her hands dirty. He'd known that. But now he'd seen it firsthand.

''Thanks,'' she said, looking up.

Bits of straw clung to her hair. Without thinking, he reached up to brush them away. Even sweat-stained and covered with straw and hay, she was beautiful. He forced himself to look away and focused on the rough-hewn beams of the barn. Darkened with age, they were silent reminders of a rugged era, of the men and women who'd struggled to survive during that time.

His thoughts took him back to Cheyenne. It wasn't difficult to picture her as a frontier woman, working the land alongside her man. She'd be a wife, a helpmate, a partner in every sense of the word.

When the silence stretched taut between them, she asked, ''Did you want something else? Other than to apologize, that is.''

He thrust the fantasy away and dragged his attention back to the present. ''I was out of line this morning. You're the professional. I had no right telling you how to do your job.''

''No, you didn't,'' she agreed.

His lips kicked up at the corners. ''Here we go again.''

"Yeah. Looks like we'll just have to agree to disagree."

A matching smiled curved her lips. "Looks like."

"Maybe I can convince you to change your mind."

"Then again, maybe you can't."

"I'm willing to take a chance. What about you?"

She hesitated, knowing he was talking about more than the training of horses. She felt the tension between them, a tension that had nothing to do with that. *All right, admit it,* she told herself. She was attracted to the man.

It was more than the fact that he had thick blond hair that reminded her of wheat ready to be harvested and a lean, rugged build that called up memories of the movie stars of her childhood. It was something much more basic. His love of the land and his understanding of Uncle Charlie touched something deep inside of her.

He flashed her one of those devastating smiles, stunning her once again. "I wouldn't say no to a cold drink."

She realized he'd been working alongside her. The heat hadn't taken a break, and neither had they. "Sorry," she said. "I didn't mean to come off like some kind of slave driver."

They headed to the kitchen, where she poured

glasses of freshly squeezed lemonade. He wandered to the far side of the room and picked up a vase from a niche carved into the corner. The vase had two openings, carefully fashioned to meet in the middle to form the body. He fingered it with something akin to awe, entranced by the delicate workmanship. "I've never seen anything like it."

"You wouldn't. It's Navajo." She took the vase from him to show him the markings on the underside.

"It's called a wedding vase. The two openings symbolize a husband and wife. The braided handle represents them joined together. Some believe that if you keep it filled with water, your union will never dissolve." She handed it back to him.

Though she'd have denied it up and down, she had a strong streak of the romantic in her. That part of her held tight to the notion that if a man and woman put flowers in a vase together, their happiness was assured. It embarrassed her more than a little that she felt that way. She preferred the practical, the logical, side of life, the side that saw hard work as the solution to all problems. But her heart still bumped a bit as she saw Burke hold the fragile vase in his big hands.

"It's beautiful," he said softly, but his gaze rested on her, a barely-there caress that made her cheeks heat with color.

''It's empty now,'' he said.

She nodded. ''There hasn't been a reason to fill it.''

''Yet,'' he added and laced his fingers with hers.

The significance of the word wasn't lost on her. She shied away from the meaning she read in his eyes and the gentleness in his touch.

''You have a wonderful home,'' he said.

''It needs a lot of work.''

His nod was accepting. ''It wouldn't be work for someone who loved it.''

She'd often thought the same thing herself. And she did love her home. But she hadn't the time or the means to indulge all that she wanted to do to the homestead.

''Someday,'' she said more to herself than to him.

''Someday.''

''Enough about me. Tell me about you.''

He lifted a shoulder. ''Not much to tell.''

''I know what you told me. You put yourself through school.''

''That's about it.''

Cheyenne knew all about going to school and working at the same time. ''It couldn't have been easy,'' she said, watching his face.

''No.'' He smiled. ''Not easy. My parents were

great. Dad drove a truck. He was gone weeks at a time. Mom always kept a candle in the window to welcome him back. One time I asked her about it. It didn't make sense when he wasn't there most of the time to see it. She told me he knew it was there. That was enough.

"There wasn't much money, but that never seemed to matter. We had a lot of love."

She felt a sharp pang of envy before pushing it aside. She didn't think about it much anymore, but sometimes, in the dark hours before night slipped into day, she still wished for . . . She shook her head, impatient with the feelings that even twenty-odd years hadn't been able to vanquish.

She found Burke looking at her with warm compassion in his eyes and flushed. A change of subject was definitely needed. "How long have you had this job?"

"Not long."

That surprised her. She figured he'd been with the Conservancy for years, and said so.

His smile was rueful as he shook his head. "I was a corporate raider. Made a pile of money, bought a condo on the waterfront, and had everything I thought I wanted."

One word snagged her attention. "Thought?"

"Yeah. I was going through the motions, but the

challenge was gone. I woke up one morning and discovered I didn't have a life. I had a job. A job that was making me miserable.''

He lifted his head to stare out at the horizon. ''What you have here, air so clean you can taste it, mountains that make you think you could reach the sky—I guess that's why I want to make it so others can enjoy it for a day or two.'' He trailed his thumb across her cheek. ''Not everyone's as lucky as you are to see it every day of their lives.''

She followed his gaze, humbled by his words. For the first time, she understood just what he was trying to do and what he had given up.

''You were really a corporate raider?''

''I had the three-piece suit, BMW, and stock portfolio to prove it.''

She couldn't imagine the life he described. ''You're happy now.''

He nodded. ''The pay's lousy, my boss wouldn't know an antelope from a cow, and there's always a pile of paperwork to do.''

''But you love it.''

''Yeah. I love it. Protecting the land and making it accessible for people who wouldn't otherwise get to experience it has always been my dream.''

''It sounds like you're making your dream come true.''

''Everyone needs a dream. What's yours?''

Cheyenne hesitated. She'd never discussed her dream with anyone, not even Uncle Charlie. "Making the ranch a paying proposition," she said. "Right now, it's self-supporting, but only just."

"There's more, isn't there?"

"There's more. But it's not likely to happen, so there's no point in discussing it."

He took her hand. "There is if you want to make it come true." At her disbelieving look, he said, "You have to say the dream out loud. At least twenty times a day. That way, you start believing it can happen."

She remained silent. She was a long way from making her dream come true.

Chapter Five

Burke felt like a thirteen-year-old boy coming to call on his best girl. The wildflowers clutched in his fist had already started to wilt.

The house rose up into the sky, its cedar siding aged to silver. A sagging porch surrounded it. Forest green shutters framed the windows. Potted plants stood as sentinels at the front door.

He sidestepped a rotting board on the porch and knocked at the door.

Uncle Charlie answered the door. Burke's disappointment that Cheyenne wasn't there was somewhat abated when Charlie invited him inside. It was a chance to learn more about the woman he was fast falling in love with.

He looked around the big living room with interest. The room was unabashedly old-fashioned. He liked that. There'd been no attempt to update it. He liked that too. It was scrupulously clean and pleasantly cluttered with pictures and trophies, most of them Cheyenne's.

Charlie spent the next few minutes telling Burke stories of Cheyenne's growing-up years.

The undisguised love in Charlie's tone made Burke smile. ''You love her a lot.''

''She is my daughter,'' the old man said simply. He placed his hand over his heart. ''In here.'' He pointed to a bronzed trophy of a rider and horse. ''Cheyenne won it in a barrel race.''

Burke lifted the trophy and noted its date. She'd have been fourteen at the time.

''Smiling Sun does not like the display of pictures and trophies. She keeps them here for me.''

''Why do you call her Smiling Sun?''

''When she was five, she had much sadness. I took her to the reservation to have the spirits bless her. The tribal elders gave her the name.''

Burke thought of the way her face lit up when she smiled. ''It fits.''

''You have given her your heart,'' Charlie said.

Burke stared at him, startled. Was he so obvious?

Charlie smiled. ''I have known Cheyenne all of her life. She is a special woman.''

''I know,'' Burke said quietly.

''You are good for her.''

Burke flushed but felt compelled to deny Charlie's implication all the same. ''She wants friendship. That's all.''

''She has changed,'' Charlie said. He gave Burke a shrewd look. ''It does not take the spirits to understand why.''

''I'm afraid you're reading a lot more into this—''

Charlie held up a hand. ''The spirits have let me know the truth.''

It seemed the old man had his own agenda. He subjected Burke to a thorough scrutiny. ''She has been hurt in the past.''

''I'd never hurt her.'' As soon as Burke said the words, he wished them back. He'd all but told her uncle that he loved Cheyenne. The sympathy in Charlie's eyes, though, convinced him he'd never betray a confidence.

''Did Cheyenne tell you I have been with the family since her father left them?'' Charlie asked, but didn't wait for an answer. ''My niece—Cheyenne's mother—asked me to come live with them a month after her husband had gone. By then she knew he would not be coming back. Cheyenne grieved like an animal, raw cries that cut through the night.'' He shook his head. ''Now she keeps her feelings close to her heart. I saw her cry only once—when I had to bury her pet lamb. Her mother held her and rocked her back and forth. After that, she never did shed a tear. Not even when her mother died. I think something died in her that day when her father left.''

Burke felt a tightening in his gut at the image of the lonely little girl, picturing the child who was the woman he loved, broken, shattered, lost.

''You will take care of her.''

Burke didn't see Cheyenne letting anyone take care of her. He said as much, earning a smile from Charlie.

''You know her well. She needs you. She pretends she does not need anyone, but Mother Earth knows differently. The wolf, the hawk both know that to be alone is not good.''

Burke tried again to set Charlie straight about the relationship between himself and Cheyenne, that she'd barely let him kiss her, but Charlie only smiled and shook his head. ''We will see.'' He stopped to stare out the window. ''My heart is there,'' he said, gesturing to the land. ''I have been bound to the house since my sickness.'' He lifted a dust cloth with a wry smile. ''This is all I am good for now.''

''You look pretty fit to me,'' Burke said, eying the older man's proud stature and strong shoulders.

''I am well. But Smiling Sun fears what will happen if I work outside.''

''She loves you.''

''Yes.'' But Charlie's eyes were sad. More than sad, Burke thought. They were resigned.

Charlie switched the subject with a swiftness that left Burke reeling. ''We have a tradition. When Mother Earth has suffered too much, a Rainbow Warrior will lead us into battle to save her.''

''I'm no warrior.''

''You see only with your eyes. You do not see with your full self. When you do, you will know the truth of my words.''

Burke only shook his head. The Rainbow Warrior had nothing to do with him.

Charlie laid a hand on his arm. ''The spirits will help you see the truth.''

''I don't know if I believe in the spirits.''

To Burke's surprise, Charlie smiled. ''You speak with honesty. That is good.''

''This Rainbow Warrior, what's he supposed to do?''

A frown blunted Charlie's brow. It was a long time before he spoke. ''Mother Earth has cycles that must be completed. When those cycles are interrupted, she chooses a brave one to come forward.''

''But what is this brave one supposed to do?''

Burke realized he was asking the question as if he bought into the whole thing.

"Mother Earth will let him know."

"How?"

Charlie's smile was back in place. "You lack patience. It is the same with Smiling Sun. She wants to run before she can crawl. But she is learning. You will learn also."

What? Burke wanted to shout. But he knew better than to rush Cheyenne's uncle. Charlie Two Feathers had his own agenda, his own timetable. It was obvious he didn't intend on saying anything more. At least not now.

"You will find Smiling Sun at the corrals."

"Keep your arms close to your sides," Cheyenne said, holding the small girl upright until she got her balance.

"Like this?"

Cheyenne smiled approvingly. "Just like that. You'll be riding out with the rest of the hands before you know it."

The dark-haired girl, Emilie Tall-Star, raised her gaze to Cheyenne's. "Do you really think so? Could I be a cowgirl with a hat and spurs and everything?"

Cheyenne patted the small shoulder and made a

mental note to find a child-sized Stetson. "I sure do. Look how you've taken to it already. You're a natural. Jenny thinks so too." She stroked the mare's neck.

Cheyenne swallowed around the tightness in her throat as she watched Emilie lean over to rub her cheek against Jenny's glossy coat.

They made a few more circles around the corral. Cheyenne stayed close, ready to step in should Emilie grow afraid. But the little girl adapted to the rocking-horse motion of Jenny's gait, all the while keeping up a steady stream of excited chatter.

"Can we go faster?"

"Sure thing." Cheyenne gave Jenny a light tap on the rump, and the mare started into a gentle trot.

"It's like flying," Emilie said, clutching the reins. "I d—didn't know anything could be l—like this. Up here, I'm just like anyone else."

Cheyenne looked at the rapt expression on the small golden face. It was one of pure joy. She knew Emilie had challenges, coping with Down's syndrome. Yet she faced each new activity with a dogged determination that Cheyenne couldn't help but envy.

They continued circling the corral for thirty minutes. Judging that Emilie had had enough for today, Cheyenne brought Jenny to a halt.

"Do we have to stop?" Emilie asked, her usual lisp practically nonexistent.

" 'Fraid so. But you'll be back next week. If you feel like it, we'll take Jenny out of the corral then."

"Can I really?"

"You betcha."

Cheyenne undid the leg straps that kept Emilie upright and then carefully lifted her down.

"I think we've got a first-rate rider in the making," Cheyenne said, giving Emilie a final hug.

"Sure looks like it," Hank said. "I'll have to watch out for my job. C'mon, Emilie. I think Uncle Charlie's got some lemonade and chocolate cake waiting for you and the rest of the kids."

Cheyenne watched as Hank herded the kids toward the house. She'd been hosting these Saturday afternoon rides for mentally challenged children from the reservation for over a year now, but the children's delight in the simple act of riding made each time seem like the first.

It hadn't been easy, convincing the social services program at the res to let her put the program into practice. At first, Cheyenne had been allowed to bring only one child. Now, she routinely brought four to six children there every Saturday.

She adored each of the kids who'd participated in the program, but there was something special about Emilie. When Cheyenne had first met Emilie, the little girl had been afraid of horses. Now, Emilie was a regular at the ranch.

Cheyenne's only regret was that she hadn't started the program years earlier. Children from the res, especially those with disabilities, faced a lifetime of doors being closed to them. Cheyenne determined that learning to ride a horse was one door that wouldn't shut in their faces. Helping these children was a small way to repay the debt she felt she owed to the reservation. With Uncle Charlie and her mother, it had become her family in the lonely years after her father had left.

She walked back to where Jenny was waiting patiently. ''You were a real lady today,'' she said, patting the mare affectionately.

She reached into her pocket and pulled out an apple. Jenny whinnied her appreciation and chewed it noisily. Cheyenne started to lead the mare to the barn to rub her down when a voice halted her.

''That was something else,'' Burke said. He was seated on the fence, long legs hooked under the lower rail.

''How long have you been here?'' she asked, wondering how much he'd seen.

''Long enough.''

Long enough for what? she wondered.

''Long enough to see that you're a fraud.''

''A fraud?''

''That's right. A fraud. You give a great performance, I'll give you that, but, inside, you're as soft as butter.''

She'd been called a lot of things but never a fraud. She wasn't sure she liked it. In fact, she was pretty sure she didn't. ''You want to explain that?''

''I like what I saw. That's all.''

Not knowing how to answer that, Cheyenne ignored it.

''That was pretty wonderful what you did with that little girl.''

Warmth that was both compassion and admiration lit his eyes and touched something buried deep inside her. Determinedly, she pushed it away. ''I took her for a ride. That's all.''

''It's not all,'' he said softly. ''You care. Maybe too much.'' Even in those few minutes, he'd seen for himself how much she cared for the little girl.

''I can't help from a distance.'' She started to lead Jenny to the barn. ''Emilie and the others need love just like other kids do.''

Burke followed. ''If you care too much, you could end up hurt.''

''If you don't care enough, it doesn't do any good.''

She lifted the saddle and blanket from Jenny and began rubbing her down, her hands moving over the horse's sleek back in rhythmic circles. She kept her eyes averted, but she felt Burke's gaze on her.

''Why didn't you tell me?'' he asked.

''I didn't know you'd be interested.'' It was a lame answer but all she could come up with.

Burke placed his hands over hers, stilling them. ''I think it's more than that. I think you were afraid I'd see something you didn't want me to.''

''That's crazy.'' Shaking off Burke's hands, she moved to Jenny's other side and repeated the process.

''Is it?''

She nodded curtly, uncomfortable with the warmth in his eyes. ''Don't make me out to be something I'm not. Once a week, I bring some children out to the ranch and give them a ride on a horse. It's not a big deal.'' She picked up a curry comb and began grooming the horse.

''It takes a special kind of person to do what you're doing. To give up your Saturdays for a bunch of kids.''

Impatient, she turned around and faced him. ''There's nothing noble about it. The kids get a kick out of it, and so do I. That's all.'' She stopped. She had no call to talk to Burke that way. No call at all. He'd only been interested, and she'd turned her temper on him. ''I'm sorry. It's just that kids from the res have a hard enough time. When they've got extra problems, it's even tougher.''

''You're protective of them.''

''Yeah. I guess I am. Kids from the res start off with one strike against them from the minute they're born.'' Her voice was quiet now, softer, without the edge that had coated it minutes ago.

He knew of the problems plaguing too many Native American reservations: unemployment, poverty, alcoholism. He had a feeling, though, that Cheyenne was talking about something else.

''Tell me,'' he said softly.

''The res can be a good place. I spent a lot of time there when I was growing up. Uncle Charlie took me. He wanted me to understand my roots. I made some friends and had fun. But I always knew I could go home at the end of the day. I didn't have to stay there day after day, go to school there, wake up there and know there was nothing else.''

''You make it sound pretty bleak.''

''Too often it is.''

''What about kids like Emilie?''

Her smile came quickly. ''Emilie was my first student. It was because of her that the tribal elders agreed to let other kids come.''

''What's . . . what's . . .'' Silently, he cursed his clumsy phrasing.

"What's wrong with her? It's all right. Emilie knows she's different. She has Down's syndrome. Her mother, Sara Tall-Star, has five other children. She has all she can do to keep her family together, especially after Emilie's father died two years ago." Her smile widened. "Emilie's got a lot of spunk. She keeps all of us on our toes."

He wondered if she knew just how much she revealed about herself when she talked about the kids. There was no mistaking the compassion in her voice. Her heart, he thought, was as big as the land, with enough room for a bunch of kids from the reservation.

"Why don't you want people knowing about it? It seems like publicity would help what you're trying to do."

"It's not a secret. Plenty of people know what we're trying to do here—doctors, counselors, social workers. Even the res can't get away without some bureaucracy." A wry smile twisted her lips. "Especially the res. But I've tried to keep it pretty low-key. If the newspapers got ahold of it, they'd be out here, taking pictures, turning it into some kind of sideshow and making the kids out to be freaks.

"All these kids need extra help. But on a horse, they're the same as anyone else."

He smiled, remembering Emilie saying the same thing only a few minutes earlier.

''That's what this is all about,'' she said. ''It's showing them that they can do anything they put their minds to.''

Burke laid a hand on her arm, his fingers warm even through the denim of her shirt. ''Your secret's safe with me.''

She looked at his clear gray eyes and knew he was telling the truth.

''Thanks.''

''You're welcome. Maybe, someday, you'd let me help you with them.''

How many times had she wished for an extra pair of hands to help with the kids? Hank and Quinn helped whenever they could, but they were usually needed elsewhere if she was to keep the ranch a paying concern. The prospect of sharing the work with Burke was a pleasant one. ''You'd do that?''

''Of course I would.'' He hesitated. ''As long as I've already put my foot in my mouth, I have another question.''

''You want to know why I didn't grow up on the reservation,'' she guessed.

''Yeah.''

''My mother's family owned property. It was deeded to her great-grandfather by the governor around the turn of the century. Over the years, they built the place up.''

''Your mother's people are Shoshone.'' At her

nod, he continued, ''How'd you end up with a name like Cheyenne?''

''When Mom was growing up, her family had a little black-and-white TV set. They didn't get many shows—the mountains don't make for good reception—just a couple of old Westerns late at night. One of them was ''Cheyenne.'' She told me she fell in love with Clint Walker when she was about fifteen years old.'' Her eyes dared him to laugh.

He smiled instead, remembering seeing reruns of the old television series. ''You run the place by yourself now.''

''With Uncle Charlie's help.''

''Maybe you ought to let him help then,'' he said mildly.

''You know why I—''

''I know you're afraid. That's no reason to keep him inside. He's dying there.''

''Did he ask you to talk to me?''

''What do you think?''

She shook her head in answer to her own question. No, Uncle Charlie would never have asked Burke to speak for him. But, now that he had, she needed to listen.

''Your uncle loves you,'' Burke said, his smile rueful.

Something in his smile encouraged one of her own. She tried it and found it felt right.

"Thanks," she said.

"For what?"

"For caring about Uncle Charlie."

"He's a great guy."

"Yeah. He is." And she had to come to terms with the fact that her uncle had chosen a virtual stranger to confide in rather than herself.

"I'll talk to him," she promised. And this time she would.

She thought of something else. If Uncle Charlie had told Burke that much, what else had he told him? She looked at Burke suspiciously. "Did he say anything else?"

Burke settled on part of the truth. "The past."

Cheyenne scowled. "Why dredge up that? The past is dead and buried."

He leaned across Jenny and caught her hands. "Is it?"

"Of course it is."

But her voice lacked conviction. He heard it, the note of pain that Cheyenne probably wasn't even aware of. His heart ached for her, for the little girl who hadn't understood her father's desertion, and for the woman who guarded her feelings so closely, afraid to let anyone too near.

He knew better than to offer any sympathy, though. He had a feeling Cheyenne wouldn't know what to do with it. He also had a feeling that she'd shut him out of her life before he got past the first word.

"Tell me about your father."

The air whooshed out of her. Whatever she'd expected, it hadn't been this. She shifted so that she wasn't looking directly at him and stared up at the sky. Was that a cloud? Rain would be an answer to her prayers and those of the other ranchers.

She lowered her gaze, uncomfortable with what she might give away with her eyes.

Burke remained silent, as though sensing her need to think through her answer. She was grateful for the time. What did she feel about her father after all these years? She'd like to be able to say that she didn't feel a thing. But that would be a lie.

She thought about all the years she'd felt driven to defend him, to downplay his desertion. With Burke, though, she no longer felt compelled to gloss over the truth. "My father left when I was five years old."

For a long time, she'd been confused. Closely on the heels of that came guilt. She'd blamed herself, wondering what she'd done to make her father leave without so much as a good-bye. If she'd been more obedient, if she'd helped more around the house, if she'd been less trouble, would he have stayed?

The questions had tormented her for years until her uncle had taken her aside and told her the truth.

Her father had left his family because he was self-ish. By then, Cheyenne had convinced herself that she didn't care.

''My father cared about two things. Himself and making money. He saw the ranch as a way to do that, saw himself as some kind of gentleman farmer.'' She laughed shortly. ''It wasn't until he figured out that running a ranch meant hard work that he took off.'' She kept her voice emotionless.

He saw the pain in her eyes and wished he had never started the story. But it was too late to stop.

''Do you ever hear from him?''

''No. Not even when my mother died.''

''How long has he been gone?''

''Twenty-three years.''

''What about your mom?''

Talking about her mother was easier. ''She was the best. She died the year I turned twelve.''

''It must have been rough on you.''

Cheyenne didn't like the soft sympathy in his voice. She wasn't accustomed to sympathy and didn't know how to deal with it. He reached out to cover her hand with his own. His fingers wrapped around hers in a wordless gesture of comfort. For long minutes, they stayed that way, neither speaking, neither feeling the need to break the silence.

At last, Cheyenne pulled her hand away, breaking the spell. She heard Burke's hiss of disappointment, but when she looked up, his eyes were filled with compassion, not the censure she halfway expected.

''I'm sorry,'' he said. ''I'm sorry it hurt you so much.''

She started to deny that she'd been hurt and then stopped herself. The simplicity of his words loosened the restraint she'd always felt whenever she talked about her parents.

''It was a long time ago.''

He took her hand again. ''Not that long.''

He was right. She could still remember the bewilderment, the pain, and the guilt she'd felt that day when she returned home from kindergarten to find her father gone. Her mother's broken explanation had only added to Cheyenne's confusion and hurt.

''It was a long time ago,'' she said again, repeating the words in an attempt to assure Burke that she was over the hurt. She couldn't bear to see the compassion in his eyes. ''I'm a big girl now.''

The pungent aroma of horses surrounded them, but suddenly Cheyenne wanted very much for him to kiss her.

Burke drew her to him. She smelled of sunshine and a faint, elusive scent that reminded him of honeysuckle.

He lowered his head. His lips met hers in a sweet

union that caused him to catch his breath. She fit him perfectly, her eyes nearly level with his.

The kiss, which he'd intended only as a light peck, stretched into seconds and then minutes. When he released her, he was trembling. Never before had a woman affected him this way.

Until now. Until Cheyenne.

The sun was riding low in the sky, all bleeding colors and fiery light, by the time he made it back to the cabin. He'd come here to try to survey the land and mark trails, but he was beginning to understand that there was much more involved than he ever realized. If he was to do his job—really do it—he needed to help find an answer for the ranchers as well as open the land to the public.

The problem gnawed at him. He couldn't stop thinking about it. Or Cheyenne. She'd become wrapped up in the problem. He told himself it was because she was a rancher, but he knew that wasn't the complete answer.

He rubbed down Traveler, taking his time and giving the gelding extra attention. The horse nuzzled his neck.

''You're just a big baby, aren't you?'' Burke crooned to the animal, giving him a final pat.

Inside, Burke pulled out a topographical map of the area. North of the range where Cheyenne and the other ranchers had been grazing their herds and flocks was a secluded spot, too inaccessible for most campers to visit, but it might be right for ranchers to pasture their animals.

Excited, he began making some calculations. He'd have to check with the Conservancy, but he had the beginnings of a plan.

He thought about Cheyenne's patience with the little girl. She'd shown a side of herself that he'd never seen before. Not that it surprised him; he'd known for some time that she wasn't as hard and tough as she made herself out to be. She was caring and compassionate, warm and generous.

She'd been uncomfortable with him witnessing the scene. He smiled, remembering how she'd lifted the little girl from the horse, settling her onto the ground with infinite gentleness. Cheyenne's hands had lingered on Emilie's shoulders as she had knelt beside the girl to whisper something to her.

He reviewed what he'd learned today of Cheyenne's childhood and felt a surge of anger toward her father, who'd denied her the security and love every child deserves. Her father had left her a legacy of distrust and fear. Burke's heart ached for the lonely little girl who blamed herself for her father's desertion. A five-year-old child shouldn't have to carry that kind of burden. Maybe, just maybe, he could teach her that feelings didn't have to be feared. Cheyenne had so much to give. If only he could convince her of it. If only she'd let him get close enough, he knew he could teach her that love didn't have to end in pain.

Cheyenne was a complex woman with as many sides as there were colors in the sky at sunset. Drawn by the idea of observing another of the spectacular Wyoming sunsets, he stepped outside. No pastels here. Vivid bands of indigo, vermilion, and pink striped the sky—bold colors, contrasting with each other, but making a perfect whole—like the woman who increasingly occupied his thoughts.

Evening sounds broke the silence: the scuffling of a small animal burrowing into the ground, the caw of a crow, and the shrill call of mating insects were each distinct, each necessary in the order of nature.

He let his mind wander, imagining he could hear another sound. . . . The sound of Cheyenne's voice reassuring the little girl as she clung to the horse. It was a sound he'd never forget.

All her reserve and cool politeness melted away when she was with the kids. It was as if they alone had the power to reach her and touch her heart. An unreasonable jealousy arose within him. Disgusted, he slammed his fist into his hand. He was jealous of a bunch of kids. He had it bad.

Like it or not, he cared about Cheyenne. He was

beginning to believe that he always would. And now that caring was perilously close to loving.

Cheyenne Roberts was the last woman he wanted to get involved with. She was feisty, irritating, and altogether exasperating. She had a mouth that wouldn't quit and a way of pushing his buttons. She was everything he didn't want in a woman. And, he had a feeling, everything he needed.

Cheyenne paused to wipe the sweat from her neck. The sound of hoofbeats made her look up. She bit back the scolding that hovered on her lips and worked up a smile as Uncle Charlie hobbled his horse.

''Aren't you supposed to be at home?'' she asked as mildly as she could.

''And do what?'' he asked bluntly. ''Make a dinner that no one will eat?'' He gave her no time to answer. ''You would tether me to the house if you could.'' There was no reproach in his voice, only sadness.

He was right. She'd found a dozen excuses why he should stay inside, why she needed him there instead of working alongside her as he always had. They'd been a team for as long as she could remember. His heart attack had ended that. Or so she thought.

Uncle Charlie lifted his gaze to where an eagle glided overhead. ''Daughter, you have kept me safe. Now you must let me soar as the eagle. Or I will die.'' He pointed to his heart. ''In here.''

Shamed, she ran to him and hugged him. ''I'm sorry. I just couldn't bear losing you.''

''As long as you love, you will never truly lose anyone.''

''I lost Mama.'' She hadn't said the words in over a dozen years.

He took her hand and placed it on his heart. ''No. When you have seen as many years as I have, you will know that you carry her here.''

Cheyenne clung to him for another moment before releasing him. ''What can I do?''

''Allow me to become the man I was,'' he said simply. ''The man I still am in here.'' He tapped his heart.

''You are.'' But she couldn't meet his eyes.

''No.'' His voice was strong, sure. ''I must go on a vision quest.''

A vision quest. She knew what it meant. A day and a night alone, spent in a circle surrounded by rocks. The person must not eat or drink or speak to another. There, he would listen to the spirits and then heed their counsel. Even young men sometimes could not stand the isolation, the intensity.

When she looked at her uncle this time, it was with her heart, instead of her eyes. And saw what she'd denied for six months.

"What can I do to help?"

His smile was her reward. "There is nothing to prepare. Do not worry. I will take care."

She wished she could be sure of that. Instead, she said the one thing she was sure of. "I love you, Uncle Charlie."

"I know."

Chapter Six

She was alone.

Uncle Charlie had gone on his vision quest. Hank and Quinn were in town, kicking up their heels and spending their paychecks.

The wind howled, a mournful lament that plucked at her nerves. Shutters banged against the house, clattering with each gust of the wind. She made her rounds of the house, starting downstairs. The first switch she turned off plunged the kitchen into darkness. Shadows appeared where there'd been light.

She'd never been uneasy in her home before and had relished those few times when she'd had the house to herself. Unaccountably, she was uneasy now.

Worry for Uncle Charlie continued to dog her. She pushed it away and headed out to the calving shed. It needed mucking out, and she needed an outlet for her feelings.

Two hours later, covered with bits of straw and smelling strongly of country sunshine, she put down the pitchfork and surveyed her efforts. The shed had never looked cleaner, which was a lot more than could be said for her, she thought with a grimace of distaste. She'd probably need sandpaper to re-move the grime.

She stepped outside and gasped. The storm, which had been brewing all day, had taken hold. Black clouds scuttled across the sky while the wind swirled dirt and gravel over the yard. Lightning speared the night. She'd been so engrossed in her work that she'd forgotten the simmering storm.

The horses, especially Silverado, would be spooked by the thunder. She started to the barn at a run.

At that moment, lightning spiked the roof of the barn. A spark caught hold and ignited a pile of straw. It all happened so quickly.

Thunder roared over the squall of the wind, ric-ocheting off the mountains and canyon walls. Not to be outdone, the wind gusted harder, blustering its way across the ranch yard. Almost blinded by the blowing grit and dirt, she groped for the latch to the barn door. She pushed at it and let herself inside.

The terrified cries of the horses galvanized her into action. She had to get to them before they injured themselves in their panic to get free.

The fire seemed to take on a life of its own, sputtering and spitting, licks of it jumping from one point to another with amazing speed. The fire spread quickly, consuming whatever stood in its way. Blue-white flames licked about her while smoke filled the air. A series of small fires erupted, separating her from the stalls.

She looked up to where a beam, weakened by the flames, teetered precariously. Too late, she realized it was falling. She sidestepped and managed to avoid the worst of it. She escaped having it land on her head and shoulders, but her legs were pinned.

She was trapped.

The storm was magnificent, a glorious, superb example of nature's fury and grandeur. Lightning jumped from one point to the next, arcing across the sky in brilliant streaks. Thunder rumbled and roared with the ferocity of a trapped beast.

He'd always been fascinated by storms, awed by the speed with which they erupted, the power they yielded. *Rain,* he thought. And was glad for

Cheyenne's sake and those of all the ranchers in the area. The air crackled with electricity, fairly snapping with it. But the hoped-for rain remained stubbornly absent.

He watched, transfixed by the intensity and violence of the raging storm.

Something was wrong.

He didn't know how he knew. It was more a feeling, a gut reaction he'd learned not to ignore. He had no reason for the uneasiness that seeped through him, but he couldn't shake the feeling that caused his neck hairs to stand at attention.

It was then that he lifted his gaze once more and saw the flames, a speck at first against the night's darkness, then a growing brightness that lit the sky. His eyes narrowed as he realized where it came from.

He was tearing across the rough ground before he finished the thought. Lightning zigzagged through the sky, and he rode a bit faster.

If the storm spooked the horses, Cheyenne could have more than she could handle. Thank goodness he had Traveler with him instead of leaving him at the ranch. Burke pushed them both, fear lodging in his throat as he remembered that Cheyenne was alone tonight at the ranch. He patted the big roan, murmuring to him as they neared the fire.

''Come on,'' he urged when Traveler balked as

the air grew acrid with smoke. He left the reins untethered on the far side of the corral, trusting the
horse to take off if need be.

The barn was a burning mass. He spared a moment to wet down his clothes with the hose con-
nected to the house, tied his wet bandanna over his
face, and then entered the barn. The terrified whin-
nies of the horses cut straight to his heart. He had
to get to them, but first he had to find Cheyenne.
He had no doubt that she was there, perhaps
trapped.

''Cheyenne!'' His voice was no more than a
croak in the smoke-thickened air. Still, he tried
again, calling her name over and over.

A grunt of pain caused him to spin around where
he saw her pinned beneath a beam. He started toward her, heedless of the flames that licked at his
feet and legs. His boots and jeans saved him from
the worst of it.

''The horses!'' she screamed over the roar of the
fire.

Their shrill cries ripped through him. He steeled
himself against them. He had to get Cheyenne out.
''Let me get you out of here first. I'll come back
for them.''

''No. Get . . .'' A paroxysm of coughing stopped
her words. ''Get . . . them . . . out.''

One look at the set of her jaw and he realized

he'd never get her to move before he saved the horses. Both cursing and praying, he started to the stalls. He opened Jenny's first. The little mare snorted, sniffing the air with her twitching nose.

''Come on, girl,'' Burke said sharply and swatted her on the rump.

Jenny needed no second urging and took off. Taffy was next. Silverado was last. He reared back when Burke opened the stall, clearly terrified. Using precious minutes, Burke threw his coat over the big gelding's head and led him out, cursing every second that passed.

He made his way back to Cheyenne. Even through the smoke, he could see the relief and gratitude in her eyes.

The beam was a supporting one, massive and unwieldy. When his efforts to lift it off her failed, he tried pulling her out from under it. His eyes watered, and he swiped at them with the corner of his bandanna. He could barely make out Cheyenne now. He reached for her hand, squeezed it, and leaned closer to hear her words over the roar of the fire.

''Get out of here.''

He didn't bother answering. There was no way he was going to leave her.

Then he saw it. It wasn't much—a metal pipe lying against the wall. What was it Archimedes had said? Give me a lever and I'll move the world.

It was growing harder to breathe. Burke dropped to his hands and knees, groping his way across the floor to the far wall. Splinters from the ruined beam bit into his hands, but he ignored the pain and focused all his energy on putting one hand in front of the other.

''Burke, get out of here!''

Cheyenne's voice, hoarse and raw, reached him, causing him to pause, but only for a moment. At last, he made it to the wall. Gulping a breath of air where the smoke was less dense, he grabbed the pipe and began retracing his path. The smoke had thickened, stinging his eyes and scraping his throat. Only the thought of Cheyenne trapped beneath the enormous beam kept him going.

When he reached her, he realized he had to stop the flames that licked along it, sputtering and crackling. In minutes, they'd reach her. He beat at them with his jacket. They snapped and spit, sparks leaping from one spot to the next, but eventually he beat back the fire that whipped its way toward her. Temporarily.

Positioning the pipe under the beam, he pushed on it with everything he had, ignoring the sting of hot metal against his hands. The beam didn't budge.

''It's no use,'' Cheyenne said between gasps.

He tried again.

The beam moved. Only a few inches, but it was enough. It had to be.

"Be ready," he shouted. He repeated the process, shifting all his weight onto the pipe and praying with everything he had.

Cheyenne inched her legs from beneath the wood. Slipping his arms around her waist, he dragged her away from the blaze. Pausing to catch his breath, he calculated the distance to the door. The fire was a greedy monster, destroying everything in its path. If he didn't act soon, it would claim them as well.

His burned hands wept with pain, but he scooped her up and started toward the door.

"I can walk," she said.

He ignored that and kept going. The doorway was engulfed with flames. He stripped off his shirt, draped it over her head, and charged through the fire. Time took on a new meaning; each second slowed to an excruciating fight through smoke and heat; distance was measured in the few feet that separated them from safety.

Outside, he collapsed onto the ground and drew in great gulps of air. Even here, he could smell the smoke, feel the heat, and taste the fear—his own.

Cheyenne was quiet. Too quiet. He shook her, gently at first, then more urgently. "Cheyenne."

"Stop shouting," she said, her voice little more than a croak. "I'm right here."

Relief shuddered through him.

She nestled into the comforting warmth of his body but couldn't stop shivering.

Ignoring the pain in his hands, Burke rubbed her arms through her shirt. ''You're freezing.''

''Not anymore.''

He rested his chin on top of her head and let his gaze sweep over the yard. The barn was a total loss, but the rest of the place had been spared. And Cheyenne was safe. Nothing else mattered, could ever matter, as much as that. Shaken by the acknowledgment, he buried his face in her hair and held her close.

Seconds bled into minutes, and still he held her. Not until she shifted a bit in his arms did he realize he might be hurting her. He willed his grip to loosen. Under the fire-lit sky, he gazed at her. Her face was soot-stained, her hair singed, her eyes red and streaming. And she was beautiful.

''You saved my life,'' she said, her voice not quite steady. Tears, dark with dirt, streaked her face. She didn't cry with the dainty, pretty tears of a movie heroine. Instead, they came in great, gulping sobs that quivered through her with such intensity that her whole body shook with them.

He hadn't a clue how to deal with a weeping woman. Tears were as foreign to him as he expected they were to her. Uncomfortable, he shifted her in his arms.

She was a strong woman, independent and feisty and stubborn. But she'd reached the end of her endurance. He saw it in her eyes, heard it in the hitch in her breathing. Right now, all he wanted was to gather her close and promise that nothing would ever hurt her again.

So he held her, murmuring the nonsense words that such situations seemed to call for. The sobs came to a shuddering stop. A hiccup, then another, signaled that the tears had ended as well.

She pulled away and scrubbed at her eyes with the back of her hands. ''Thanks for letting me get it out.''

''I'd say you needed to. Anyone would.''

''And you didn't make me feel like too much of a wimp. So, thanks.'' She was as awkward at dealing with her embarrassment as he'd felt in coping with her tears.

It was endearing, he thought, the way the soft color stained her cheeks. Even with the dirt and soot, he could detect the blush that heightened her already exotic coloring.

Gently, she drew him to her, careful to not touch his hands. ''I'll never be able to thank you. If it hadn't been for you, the horses . . .'' Her voice faltered, failed. She drew a steadying breath. ''I couldn't bear it if anything happened to them.''

Even now, when she'd nearly lost her life, she thought of the animals first. He shook his head, trying to understand this woman who had captured his imagination. And his heart.

''I'm not letting anything happen to you,'' he said. ''You're too important.''

She laid her head against his shoulder. It felt good, he decided. More, it felt right. He'd analyze that later. For now, it was enough that they were alive.

''Could we stay this way . . . just for a minute?'' she asked.

He knew what it must have cost for her to ask that and tightened his arms around her.

Sirens sliced through the night. He welcomed the arrival of the paramedics, knowing Cheyenne was suffering from smoke inhalation, plus a leg that was probably sprained, or perhaps broken.

They wanted to tend to his hands, but he directed them to Cheyenne first.

He watched as they loaded her into the ambulance. When she started to protest, he bent over her. ''I'll be along.''

''Okay, buddy, your lady's being taken to the hospital,'' one of the paramedics said. ''Your turn. Let's take a look at those hands.''

They *were* hurting, Burke admitted silently. He didn't protest as they were wrapped in gauze.

At the county hospital, his hands were treated, and the doctor pronounced that his burns were only first-degree. "You were lucky. You'll be hurting for a while, but it should go down pretty quick." He gave Burke a prescription for painkillers and instructions to take it easy.

Burke barely heard him in his anxiety to find Cheyenne. He stopped a nurse and said, "The lady who was brought in a few minutes ago. I have to see her."

"The doctor's with her."

He paced the hallway, impatient and ready to take the head off anyone who got in his way.

When the doctor left, the nurse told Burke he could see Cheyenne. "But only for a minute," she said. "She's pretty woozy from the painkillers."

Her face was drained of color, her eyes dark and shadowed against the unaccustomed pallor of her skin. But she smiled as she saw him. "Thank you."

"We've already been through that," he muttered.

"You're a hero," she murmured sleepily. "My hero."

"There's something I've been wanting to do all night," he said. And lowered his head to kiss her.

I love you. The words echoed through his mind. The time was coming when he wouldn't be able to keep the feelings—or the words—to himself. They were as much a part of him as breathing. She'd fight them. And him. She was as independent as that little mare she was so fond of. And twice as stubborn. He loved her in spite of it. Or maybe, he thought with an inward grin, because of it.

She was troubled. He knew it, accepted it. She had yet to say the words he longed to hear. That would come in time.

For now, he was content to savor this moment.

The nurse entered, smiling as she saw the kiss. ''Time's up,'' she said to Burke.

Reluctantly, he left the room.

Hands bandaged, he felt clumsy and slow as he tried to sign the forms necessary for his release. He shuddered at how close he'd come to losing Cheyenne. He was in love with her. There was no doubt about it. The speed with which he'd fallen only intensified his feelings for her.

He hadn't come to Wyoming looking for love, hadn't figured it as part of his immediate future. But it was here—full-blown and overpowering. Now that he'd found it, he wasn't about to turn his back on it.

He loved her.

He longed to hear the same words from her. But it was no good asking. Those words had to be freely given, out of her need, not his.

He knew he'd have a fight on his hands. Cheyenne was as skittish as a newborn filly when he started to get too close. He'd find a way past her fears, he promised himself. She'd been vulnerable tonight, shaken by what had happened, by what had almost happened. He had a feeling by the following day, though, she'd slip back behind the walls she'd so carefully constructed around her.

With promises to the doctor that she'd take it easy and stay in bed, Cheyenne was allowed to go home in two days. Uncle Charlie had picked her up and brought her home. She was at once relieved and disappointed that Burke hadn't accompanied him. When she casually asked about him, Uncle Charlie said that Burke had something he had to do.

He must have sensed some of her disappointment. ''The Rainbow Warrior cares for you.''

Uncle Charlie didn't know what he was talking about. Much as she wanted to deny it, he was an old man and prone to imagining things. Obviously his illness was causing him to see something between Burke and Cheyenne that wasn't there.

She knew she'd blundered. Turning to Burke had been a mistake of monumental proportions. She'd been fragile, defenseless, weepy. She flushed, recalling how she'd cried on his shoulder. Now that she was feeling more her usual self, she was mortified at having him witness her weakness.

It had been years since she'd allowed herself to be that vulnerable, to lean on another human being. She hated the neediness on her part. It reminded her too keenly of the way she had clung to her uncle when her father had abandoned her mother and herself. Granted, she had been hurting and scared in the aftermath of the fire, but that didn't mean she had a right to turn to Burke, to draw on his strength when her own was lacking. It had been an instinctive reaction, one she didn't question or try to analyze. For once, her heart, not her head, had been in control. The realization was a sobering one.

Burke had been gentle, as she'd known he would, his touch surprisingly tender for such a big man. She frowned, remembering her reaction to that touch. Burke had found his way past the barriers she'd kept firmly in place for over two decades. He'd done it so easily, so naturally that she hadn't even noticed.

All her adult life, she had depended on herself. She didn't intend to change that now. It was time to reestablish the boundaries, to make it clear that while she appreciated his support, his friendship, that was all there was between them, all there could be between them.

When Burke checked in on her, she was cool, polite, and reserved. He should have known, had halfway expected it, but he still couldn't stifle his disappointment. He recalled Cheyenne's discomfort when she'd cried on his shoulder. It had been more than simple embarrassment over a few tears. She'd never learned to express her feelings and was uneasy when she couldn't control them.

''Thank you again,'' she said, the stiff formality in her voice causing his lips to tighten.

''I just did what you'd have done for me.'' He fit a finger beneath her chin to lift her gaze to his. The closed expression smarted more than the burns on his hands.

He wasn't surprised. Not really. But he was disappointed. After all they'd been through, she'd pulled back into herself with no hint remaining of the woman who'd opened up to him. She had withdrawn from him as effectively as if she'd built a wall between them.

It was deliberate. Perhaps that was what hurt the most, the realization that she knew what she was doing and felt compelled to do it anyhow.

He shouldn't care, but it was too late for that, far too late. He wanted to stalk away, to nurse his wounded heart. Then he noticed the faint shadows beneath her eyes, giving her a bruised and fragile look. Her skin had lost its usual glow and was pale against the dark curtain of her hair.

''You're not easy,'' he said. ''You only let me go so far before you start backing away.''

''I have reasons—''

''I know. I know. I guess it's just up to me to change your mind.''

He threw the words down as a challenge. Or a threat.

But the lips he touched to hers were gentle. He didn't need to coax a response from her. It came as easily as breathing, as naturally as a flower lifting its face to the sun. She was trembling when he raised his head.

''You . . . me . . .''

''Yeah,'' he said in a husky voice. ''You and me.'' Tenderly, he brushed the graze on her temple. His fingers felt like rough silk against her skin.

He left her alone for the rest of the day. She needed time, and so did he, to adjust to what was happening between them. He'd find a way to reach her. Time was on his side . . . and determination.

Cheyenne drummed her fingers against the desk she'd asked Uncle Charlie to set up in her bedroom.

He and Burke had ganged up on her, insisting she stay inside and rest her leg for the rest of the week. Even Hank and Quinn had joined in. She couldn't fight the four of them. In truth, she didn't feel like fighting. Her leg throbbed. And her throat was still painful from smoke inhalation.

Silently, she cursed her injured leg. If not for that, she'd have been out there with them, working to clear away the debris of the ruined barn and deciding what, if anything, could be saved. What she really needed, she decided, was a ride, feeling the wind whip through her hair, instead of being stuck behind a desk with her leg propped up on a stool. Not that she was accomplishing much, she acknowledged ruefully.

As long as she couldn't help with the barn, she'd decided to work on the books. She'd stared at the same set of figures for the last two hours without making any progress in sorting them out. She rationalized her inability to concentrate with the thought of her injured leg. It *did* hurt, but she knew it was more than the pain that kept intruding on her work. It was something much more elemental and far more disturbing . . . the memory of Burke's touch.

She pushed her hair back, her fingers encountering the scrape along her temple. Memories of Burke soothing that same spot caused her to pause.

By the end of the third day, she was cross at the inactivity and more worried than she wanted to admit. Her thoughts kept returning to the barn. How was she supposed to rebuild it? Even with the insurance check, she'd be short of the cash she needed for all the materials, not to mention labor. She struggled to bury the worry, but it nagged at her unmercifully.

She had friends she could call on for help, but they had their own work. She couldn't impose upon them. She knew Uncle Charlie and Burke and the others were sorting through the mess even now.

When Burke and Uncle Charlie had the misfortune to check on her, she snapped at them. ''Tell him, Uncle Charlie,'' she said. ''Tell him that I don't need to be babied.''

She should have known better than to look to help from that quarter. Uncle Charlie merely smiled, bent to place a kiss on her forehead, and left, a small smile on his lips. Ever since he'd returned from his vision quest, he'd moved with new dignity.

''Here,'' Burke said, holding two pills in one hand and a glass of water in the other.

''Not yet.'' She wasn't ready to take the pain medication. The label listed drowsiness as one of the possible symptoms. And she couldn't afford that, not right now. She needed all her wits about her when Burke was near.

''Now.''

"I've got—"

"They can wait." The calm reasonableness in his voice irritated her.

"But—"

"Your leg. It's hurting, isn't it?"

"No," she lied even as a twinge of pain nagged at her.

"Liar."

Reluctantly, she nodded. "Maybe a little."

He studied her face. "Try a lot."

"Okay. It hurts a lot."

"Was that so hard to admit?"

"Yeah." Seeing the stubborn set to his lips, she popped the pills into her mouth, then made a face at him. "Satisfied?" She picked up an insurance report on the fire, intending to go over it once more.

"I will be as soon as you're back in bed where you belong."

"Just let me finish—"

Burke took the papers from her. "Uh-uh," he said. "Later. You're staying in bed."

Her head felt woozy; her heart was racing. She wanted to blame it on the pills, but she had a feeling it had more to do with Burke's hands on hers. "I'm not thinking straight."

"That's because you need a decent night's sleep. Some food. And a break."

''I have a ranch to tend to.''

''We'll see to it.''

Burke made good on his promise. He also found a way to make grazing pastures available to the ranchers without sacrificing the land he was sent to turn into a national park. He was, she realized, a man a woman could count on.

The admission brought a frown to her face. She didn't want to count on any man. Uncle Charlie was the only man in her life. She liked it that way.

Chapter Seven

The colors had deepened as autumn edged closer to winter. The sun still burned brightly, but the days had grown shorter, the nights longer. Deer foraged closer to the ranch, looking for food. After the days of inactivity, restlessness built within Cheyenne.

She thought of the myriad chores that had piled up while she had been laid up. The men had nearly completed the barn. She'd itched to be outside, watching. Helping, she admitted to herself. She wanted to be a part of it.

Burke had been adamant in his refusal to let her see the barn until it was done. When he came in to escort her to what he referred to as ''the unveiling,'' she was as excited as a child on her first day of school.

The new barn sparkled under its coat of fire-engine red paint. She walked around it slowly, marveling at the careful tongue-and-groove construction, and the sturdy stalls smelling of fresh hay.

She turned to the group of men, from both the reservation and town, who had helped put up the barn in record time. ''I can't ever thank you enough.''

''There is no need.'' Sam Raven, long-time neighbor and friend, tipped his hat back. ''You are family.''

They shared no blood, only a heritage of working and loving the land. ''You would do the same for us.'' He gestured to the other men gathered around.

They gave embarrassed grunts of assent.

She nodded. He was right. Helping a neighbor in need was as ingrained as was caring for the land. Each was a stewardship.

''You have a good man there.'' Sam nodded his head in Burke's direction.

''He's not—''

''He is the Rainbow Warrior,'' Uncle Charlie said, joining them.

''He's a friend,'' she said firmly. ''That's all.''

Uncle Charlie and Sam exchanged a long look

that she didn't try to decipher. Instead she wandered over to Burke, who was standing slightly apart from the others.

She laid a hand on his arm. "I don't know what to say."

"Then don't say anything."

"I have to thank you."

"I don't want your thanks."

"What do you want?" She didn't expect him to have an answer. She should have known better.

"Let me help around here a while longer."

Pride, automatic and intense, kicked in. "You already have."

"I have some personal days coming. I'd like to spend them with you."

"You want to spend your days off mending fence, baling hay, and tending sick animals? Doesn't sound much like a vacation to me."

"Depends on where you're standing. It sounds just fine to me."

It did to her too.

"Friends?" Tentatively, she stuck out her hand.

"Friends." His fingers wrapped around her own, strong, comforting, and reassuring.

Everyone left soon after that with a great deal of good-natured advice that she was to take it easy and keep out of trouble.

Cheyenne couldn't deny that she was looking forward to spending time with Burke. Now that they'd resolved their feelings for each other, they could enjoy each other's company without fighting. *Friends,* she thought in relief. A person could never have too many friends. That settled, she relaxed.

Things changed after that. More precisely, she changed.

She smiled and thought how comfortable she was with Burke. In the space of only a few weeks, they'd found each other's rhythms, their comforts, and understood their likes and dislikes. She didn't delude herself into believing that there was anything more than friendship between them—she wouldn't let there be. She'd learned her lessons well.

But she was starting to depend on him, a dangerous position for a woman. Depending on a man—any man—was foolish.

Burke had taken to spending Saturday afternoons at the ranch, helping her with the riding program. Right now he was coaching a small boy with cerebral palsy.

"You two make a mighty pretty couple," Hank said while she and Burke worked with the kids from the reservation. "He's good with them."

"Don't you have some work to do?" she snapped.

Hank gave her a puzzled look. "Sure, Boss."

She'd just bitten Hank's head off when he'd done nothing more than make an innocent comment. She'd apologize later, she promised herself. Hank was a good friend and deserved better.

''You've got it bad,'' she muttered to herself. She had no right taking out her frustration on Hank or anyone else. The simple truth was that she was afraid—afraid of what Burke was doing to her. She was also more than a little attracted to him. But that was it. It had to be. There was no room in her life for a man, except on a friendship basis.

She'd felt the subtle shift in their relationship as they'd worked alongside each other the last two weeks. When she'd invited him to the ranch on the weekend to help with the riding program, she'd felt as carefree and happy as one of the children.

She needed time, she told herself, time to step back, put some distance between herself and Burke. She'd allowed things to move too quickly, too intensely. That would have to change. A woman who fell in love nearly overnight couldn't trust herself, or her feelings. It was time to inject some logic into the situation.

She was drawn to Burke in a way that defied logic. He was everything she shouldn't want, everything she didn't *want* to want. How could she let herself, even for a moment, think that he might be the man for her?

Was he? Wrong for her? She'd believed herself to be in love once before. It had been so long ago that she was hard-pressed to picture his face. He'd been about to graduate from college, and was working on his thesis on the reservation as a subculture. She'd shown him around, introduced him to the tribal leaders, and spent every available moment with him.

He'd been attentive, flatteringly so. And gentle. She'd craved that. How much, she hadn't known until Terry had come into her life.

When he'd finished with his paper, he'd kissed her good-bye and told her it had been fun. Fun. She'd fallen in love with him, and he had called it "fun." Her heart had shut down after that, and with it, her ability to trust.

She'd vowed then to keep her heart whole.

Burke had taken off soon after the children left. Cheyenne missed him already. She forced her attention back to the monthly report. The ranch was operating in the black—by a narrow margin, to be sure, but at a profit all the same. If she could only keep it that way for the next few months, they'd be in good shape for the next season. Then she worked her way through the tax forms that had to be filled out, in triplicate, but her mind was far away.

Cheyenne kept at it for another hour, paying bills

and balancing the books. At last, she shoved his chair back and stood. The hours of sitting at the desk had caused her legs to cramp. She grimaced as she pushed herself to her feet, a thousand needles stinging her legs. Maybe a short walk outside would ease the soreness. A few minutes in the fresh air . . . The thought went unfinished as Uncle Charlie walked in.

''You worry over the money,'' he said with a frown at the bills littering the desk. ''The hospital. Doctors. Because of me.''

She gave a forced smile. ''You're not the only one who can run up bills around here.'' She pulled an invoice for feed for the stock from the pile. ''See?''

''I see a daughter who tries to do everything.'' He took her hand in his gnarled ones. ''I see one who works too hard to care for those she loves.''

She gave him a quick hug, humbled, as always, by what he gave her—love, unconditional and overwhelming. Whatever she was, whatever she achieved, it was largely due to him.

''The hawk has a mate,'' he said. ''Even the lone wolf has a mate. Man is no different. Or woman.''

Unbidden, pictures of Burke intruded into her thoughts. He'd make a good husband and father, she decided. He had the right blend of softness and strength, compassion and humor to cope with the demands of raising a family. She had no doubt that when he committed himself, it would be forever.

Impatiently, she pushed the thought away. She had no right thinking of Burke in those terms. No right at all.

Then why did it feel so *right*?

By the following morning, she was no nearer to finding an answer than she had been the night before.

Burke rapped on the kitchen door before she'd even had her first cup of coffee. He eyed her riding clothes. ''Good. You're all ready.''

''Ready for what?''

''We're going on a picnic.''

She had a dozen things to do. She rattled them off, only to have Burke wave them away. ''We'll get to them later,'' he said.

''Burke, this is important. I have to . . . What did you say?''

''We're going on a picnic.''

A picnic. A mental picture of spending the day with Burke was unexpectedly appealing. ''But the chores—'' she felt bound to protest.

''Can wait. Today's a picnicking day.''

''What's a picnicking day?''

He pulled open the kitchen door. ''Look. Feel.''

She looked. And felt.

They day sparkled. Sun shimmered off the tin

roof of the calving shed. A breeze, no more than a puff of air, found its way through the open door. The heavy scent of newly harvested wheat scented the air.

Burke was right. The day was begging for a picnic. Whatever else happened, she would have this day with him. Nothing would spoil it, she promised herself. This would be their day, one for her to look back upon and cherish.

''Give me five minutes,'' she said.

She returned within the allotted time, anxious to start their day. Today belonged to the two of them. There'd be time enough later to worry over the differences that separated them.

''Are you ready?'' Burke asked, untying Traveler's reins from the fence railing.

''Almost. I just wanted to give Taffy an apple.'' Cheyenne handed the piece of fruit to the mare, who gobbled it down greedily.

''You spoil her,'' he said.

''I suppose you don't spoil Traveler?''

He laughed. ''You got me.''

As though aware that he was the topic of conversation, Traveler snorted and pranced about.

Burke patted the big gelding's neck. ''I know, boy. You don't like to be kept waiting, do you?'' He flashed Cheyenne a teasing smile. ''That's what happens when you're taking a lady out, though.''

She made a face at him, but her heart was light. The day promised to be one of those rare summer days when the heat didn't climb into the triple digits, and the breeze was cool rather than stinging.

''Let me help you up.'' He checked the length of the stirrups, and, satisfied, gave her a boost up on Taffy. He mounted Traveler, whispering to the gelding in a conspiratorial manner.

Cheyenne could have sworn the big horse nodded in agreement.

They kept the pace slow so they could enjoy the scenery. Wildflowers cropped up in unexpected places, spots of brilliant color against the sun-seared ground. In spite of the drought, the land held its own kind of beauty, one filled with stark contrasts. The sky, as though to make up for the arid ground, was a vivid, cloudless blue.

They encountered a rough stretch of ground, and Taffy neighed in protest as Cheyenne pulled tighter on the reins. ''Sorry, girl.''

She chanced a look back at Burke. He looked totally at home on a horse, as comfortable in the setting as she was herself. The gaze he shot back at her was steady and clear, radiating integrity and strength.

When they reached flat ground, she let Taffy have her head. ''Race you to the trees,'' she challenged

Burke, pointing to a stand of firs about a hundred yards away.

She slapped Taffy's side and took off hard. If she could outrace him, maybe she could also outrace her unruly feelings and wayward heart. Traveler had the advantage of size. But Taffy had heart. With Cheyenne's lighter weight, they beat Burke and his mount by a nose.

Breathless, Cheyenne dismounted and leaned against a tree, her chest heaving. Burke joined her. But it was more than exertion that had her heart stumbling against her chest. It was him.

She swiped at the perspiration that trickled down her neck. When he suggested they stay there for lunch, she was glad to comply. She saw to the horses while Burke opened his saddlebags and spread out the picnic.

Cheyenne looked at the array of food and whistled. "You've got enough here to feed an army."

"Uncle Charlie volunteered to pack the food. I guess he didn't want us to run short."

They'd be lucky to put away half of what was in front of them, she thought. "We could share with Traveler and Taffy."

"No way. They've got their own food."

She followed his gaze to where the horses chomped on the grain that she had brought for them.

She and Burke took their time eating, teasing each other over who had put away the most food.

''Since I brought lunch,'' he said, ''I'll let you clean up.''

She gave him a pained look. ''Thanks.''

He stretched out, using his jacket to pillow his head, and watched as she repacked everything into the saddlebags. When she was satisfied that the area was spotless, she squatted down beside him.

She looked different today, Burke thought, more carefree. Maybe it was getting away from the ranch and all the responsibilities that went with it. He knew she loved what she did, but the work was backbreaking and never-ending. He guessed she didn't take many days off, if any. Until now.

He flexed his hands, deliberately drawing her attention to them. ''Do you have to get back right away?''

''Are your burns still giving you trouble?'' she asked, concern creasing her forehead.

''A bit.''

''You should have said something. . . . We didn't have to go out today.''

''No. It did me good to get away. That's why I was asking . . .'' He let his voice trail off.

''No. I don't have to get back right away.''

''Good.'' He turned away before she saw the satisfied smile that settled on his lips. He'd played upon her sympathies shamelessly. And he'd do it again if it meant she'd take some time off. She'd been working flat-out ever since she'd returned to work.

She enjoyed being with him. The realization was a heady one. Most women wouldn't be content to spend the day under the scorching sun with nothing more exciting planned than looking at the scenery. But then, Cheyenne wasn't most women.

''I told you my dream. What's yours?'' he asked.

She'd never put words to her dream before, not even to herself. The idea scared her, but it tugged at her as well. She suddenly wanted to say the words aloud, to test them. She looked at Burke and knew there was no one else with whom she'd rather share it.

''I want to turn the ranch into a place for children with disabilities. Full time.

''It'd take money,'' she said with a long sigh. ''Lots of money. More than I could put together for a long time, the way things are going right now.''

''What would you have to do to start making the kind of money you'd need?''

''We'd have to breed more sheep and cattle, probably hire on a couple more hands.''

He uncurled his hand from hers and cupped her face.

"It's a wonderful dream, Cheyenne. You'll make it happen."

"What makes you so sure?"

"I believe that dreams can come true. If you want something enough, you'll find a way to make it happen."

She wanted to believe him. She wanted it more than she could remember wanting anything. But life had taught her some hard lessons, ones she wasn't likely to forget.

They were quiet now. It was a good kind of silence, the kind that gave a person room to think . . . to feel. She didn't feel the need to fill it with chatter. Burke was easy to be with. Like now, he was content to simply be with her and absorb the beauty around them.

Burke looked down at her and smiled. Her eyes were closed, her face tilted up to catch the sun. She didn't have a smidgin of makeup on, her hair was ruthlessly pulled back at her nape, she wore faded jeans and a shirt that had seen better days . . . and she was the most beautiful woman he'd ever known.

"We're a lot alike, you know," he said.

Cheyenne lifted her head and pulled away. Her breathing was not quite steady.

Were she and Burke alike?

At one time she'd have denied it emphatically. But now, she wasn't so sure. He was committed to his job. So was she. He fought for what he believed. So did she. He loved the land. So did she. He . . .

The list went on until she was shaking her head. He'd found a way through the defenses she'd built. But that didn't mean that she felt anything more for him than the appeal that a woman feels for an attractive man.

He was more than attractive. He was also smart, funny, and articulate. He challenged her, made her think and question things. No other man had ever affected her that way. She had an uneasy feeling no man ever would again.

''Daydreaming?'' he teased, ending her air of abstraction.

She felt her cheeks heat with color. ''Yeah. A bit.''

''Me too.'' His look was unmistakable. ''About you. About doing this.''

The kiss was sweet, unbelievably so. And tender, unbearably so. It was everything a kiss should be, everything she dreamed it might be, everything she knew it could be. And still it stunned her.

She'd never known a man could give so much, nor that she was so greedy. His lips were everywhere—behind her ear, across her brow, finally finding the sensitive spot at the hollow of her throat. He was a magician.

She gave herself up to the moment.

His hand splayed across her back, his touch sending a wave of elation roiling through her. She arched closer. His hand worked its way upward until his fingers came in contact with the soft skin of her upper arms. She shivered tremulously at his touch and felt her heart contract painfully.

Burke drew her to him even more closely, as though he could keep out the rest of the world. For those moments, there was only the two of them. With her head cradled in the slight curve of his shoulder, she was aware of only him and the awareness humming between them. A sigh of sheer contentment escaped her lips.

He felt her every shift and move, heard the hitch in her breathing, saw the warmth in her eyes. Emotion flooded through him, and his heart leapt with love. The setting wasn't designed for romance: a few straggly trees to provide shade; summer-dried grass, dotted with wildflowers, carpeted the area. A jagged ridge of rocks bordered it. But it produced a feeling of lazy contentment that he was loath to leave.

It couldn't last. He knew it. But he wasn't above taking advantage of this time, this respite from the pressures that separated them. He loved her.

''I had a wonderful time,'' she said and turned to him, her eyes shining with happiness. ''Thank you for making it happen.''

''Hey, it was a joint effort. You and me. We make a pretty good team, don't we?''

He waited. More depended upon her answer than he wanted to admit. She was the one woman he could see spending the rest of his life with.

She nodded. ''I think you know how I feel.''

''No . . .''

He cupped her shoulders, bringing her close enough that he could smell the minty scent of her breath. He inhaled deeply and knew this scent would be forever imprinted on his memory. ''I love you.''

He wouldn't exaggerate, she knew. It wasn't his style. His were simple words said with simple truth.

Cheyenne shivered. It wasn't the sudden chill of the wind, though, that made goosebumps pucker her flesh. It was the promise of permanence she saw in Burke's eyes, the warmth that flooded the usually cool gray.

It scared her.

He drew her to him and cupped her cheek. ''Marry me.''

Chapter Eight

‘‘Wh . . . what did you say?’’

‘‘Marry me.’’

‘‘Just like that?’’

‘‘Just like that.’’ He picked her up and twirled her around. ‘‘Make me the happiest man alive.’’

Breathless, she steadied herself against him after he lowered her to the ground. Her heart was doing somersaults, but not from joy. A dozen emotions raced through her. Dominating them all, though, was fear.

She didn't speak, didn't dare to. What threatened to come out was *yes,* and she feared that most of all.

A pressure built in her chest, a weight that felt

141

very much like pain. She couldn't breathe, then realized she'd been holding her breath. Slowly, deliberately, she let it out. That would ease the pressure, she hoped.

It didn't.

She'd known a long time ago that love wasn't in the plans for her, but a life with a man whom she both cared about and respected was more than appealing. He looked at her, his heart in his eyes, and she was tempted, yes, tempted to accept what he offered. She almost managed to convince herself that it would be all right.

When he placed his hands on her waist, she closed her eyes. Why hadn't she seen this coming? Maybe she had and she'd simply ignored it. For a man like Burke, love would lead to marriage. He was too honorable to settle for anything else.

''Cheyenne.'' His voice was gentle, but she could hear the underlying impatience and frustration.

She looked up at him, longing to give him the answer he wanted and knowing that she couldn't.

''I wasn't sure what you'd say,'' he said, his chin resting on her head, ''when I asked you.''

He felt, more than heard, the sharp intake of breath. And he was afraid.

He fit a finger beneath her chin, needing to see her face. ''I love you, Cheyenne.'' He waited. Hoping. Praying.

She framed his face with her hands. ''I care about you, Burke. You know that.''

He nodded.

''I care about you more than I ever dreamed possible.''

Still, he waited. When the silence became unbearable, he filled it with a rush of words.

''I want to spend the rest of my life with you. I'll always take care of you.'' He spread his hands, the gesture encompassing the windswept range. ''I've fallen in love with you and your beautiful country.''

''I . . . I appreciate that.'' She placed her hand on his heart. It thudded against her palm, racing, straining. She knew if she felt her own, it would feel the same.

''I need you, Cheyenne. More than I thought I'd ever need any woman, anyone.''

His breath hitched as he waited.

''I love you.'' He said the words fiercely, as though by sheer force of will he could make her accept the truth of them, the rightness. He took her hand, linking his fingers with hers. He looked down at their joined hands. They fit so well, he thought. Just slid together, as if they'd been made for that sole purpose. Why couldn't she see it?

Gently, she freed herself. ''Burke, I care about you. You have to believe me. I've never said those things to another man. Except Uncle Charlie.''

Moved by the rough emotion in her voice, he nodded. "I know that."

"I'm trying to be totally honest with you. I'd do anything for you. Anything, but . . ."

A new fear gripped him as he started to understand. "Anything but say you love me. Is that it?" He willed her to deny the words, to laugh away his fears, to let him take her in his arms and tell her that she loved him as much as he loved her. But a look at her eyes confirmed what he'd already known.

He gripped her shoulders. "Why can't you let go of the past?" Pain squeezed his heart. "I love you. All you have to do is believe it."

She did. Heaven help her, she did. How could she not, when his eyes caressed her, and her heart bumped against her chest in a race to reach the safe haven he offered?

"I have to know." He took a breath and asked the most important question he'd ever ask. "What am I to you?"

"You're my friend," she said, the hitch in her voice going straight to his heart.

Friendship was a tepid term for what he felt for her. "It's not enough anymore. Since the fire . . . since I almost lost you, things are different. Life's too short to waste a single moment. I want to spend the rest of mine with you."

"I never lied to you."

"Nope." He laughed shortly. "You never lied to me."

"I thought we had an understanding." Desperation laced her voice, desperation and fear.

He heard it, understood it, and hated himself for causing it. "No. *You* had an understanding. You made the rules. You called the plays. And I wanted to be with you so much that I let you do it."

"There are some things I can't give." She reached for his hands.

"Can't or won't?"

"What's the difference?"

He shook off her hands. "I could be your best friend. But if you can't say the words, nothing will ever be enough. Don't you understand?" He wanted to reach out and snare a fistful of the dark hair, urging her toward him. But he kept his hands to himself, knowing if he touched her, he wouldn't be able to let her go.

He shoved a hand through his hair instead. "I've offered you everything I have, everything I am, and you throw it back at me because you're afraid."

"I have a right—"

"Don't throw that garbage at me again. Plenty of kids have fathers who walk out on them. They manage to survive, to grow up, and fall in love and get married and have kids of their own. What makes you think you're so special?''

She flinched at the harshness of his words.

He'd been deliberately cruel, trying to shake her out of the past.

''I love you.'' He threw the words out. ''I love you,'' he said again, more gently this time. ''You're everything I ever wanted, and I mean to have you.

''I won't walk out on you.'' He saw the trace of understanding in her eyes. ''I won't let you down.'' He paused, letting his words sink in. ''And I won't leave you.''

''How can I be sure?'' she asked, so softly he almost missed it.

''Because I love you.''

She wanted to return the words. He saw it in the trembling of her lips, the darkening of her eyes.

''Can't we keep on as we have been?'' she asked at last.

He looked at her and, for a moment, almost relented, his resolve threatening to crumble at the pain he saw in her face. He steeled himself against the plea in her eyes and knew he was going to destroy whatever was between them.

For a heartbeat in time, he'd been tempted. Friendship was a bland substitute for what he felt for her, but he wondered if half a loaf was better than none at all. He hadn't taken it because he wanted more. A lot more.

The hope faded from her eyes as the silence between them stretched taut. They now wore the shuttered look he'd noticed when he first met her, the look they assumed whenever she was afraid of showing what she felt. He'd have to live with the knowledge that he'd done that.

"You know what's ironic?" he asked. "You already love me. I see it in your face. I feel it when you touch me. But you can't say the words. You can't force yourself to say the words because if you did, you'd be vulnerable like the rest of us. And that's the one thing you won't allow yourself to be."

He saw the denial in her eyes. Even now she was lying to him, to herself, he reflected sadly. "When you decide to stop living in the past and step into the future, you know where I'll be." He fought to keep his hands to himself, desperate to have her back in his arms.

He mounted Traveler and picked up the reins. "I love you, Cheyenne. I always will. Nothing's going to change that. Not even you."

He shored up his determination. There'd be another day, he promised himself. A true warrior knew when to stay and fight and when to retreat.

''Good-bye, Cheyenne.'' He clung to the horse's reins and resisted the urge to look back. If he did, he wasn't sure he'd have the strength to leave.

He wondered if he'd been a fool for not taking what she'd offered, and, for a moment, he wavered. Would it be so wrong to settle for friendship? She loved him. He knew it. In time, he could teach her that love could heal the pain she was carrying inside. He had love enough to wait while she accepted her own feelings.

He shook his head in answer to his question.

Unless Cheyenne could accept that he loved her, unless she could allow herself to be vulnerable by admitting her love, they didn't have a future. And he loved her too much to accept half a life.

Cheyenne stared after him as he rode off. She wanted to go after him, but if she gave into that need, she might say what she didn't mean, what she didn't believe in, wasn't ready for.

Words to call him back hovered on her lips. She'd say the words he longed to hear, and everything would be all right. Even as the thought formed, she knew she couldn't do it.

She was alone. Bitterly alone with only her thoughts for company. She dug her nails into her palms. A burning sensation began somewhere deep inside her, and she recognized it as the beginning of pain.

He'd asked for too much.

It took seven days a week, sixteen hours a day to keep Sweet Water running. It demanded that she sacrifice everything she had, everything she was, everything she might have been, just to hold onto it. It was a constant struggle, and one she'd gladly perform for the rest of her life.

But it hadn't demanded more than she could give. Love was a crippling emotion, one that drained the strength and energy from anyone foolish enough to believe in it.

Burke was wrong. He'd asked for the one thing she couldn't give.

This was ridiculous.

A week later, Cheyenne was drumming her fingers on her desk. Why was she sitting here in her office, staring at the walls, and feeling like everything in her life had lost its meaning?

The important things, the things that made her who she was, what she was, were still intact: Uncle Charlie, the kids from the res, the ranch. Then why did she feel like a boat whose mooring lines had all been cut? She turned back to the stack of bills, but again, her attention strayed.

The sight of Burke's angry face the last time she'd seen him had imprinted itself upon her mind. She remembered the warmth of his lips as he'd

kissed her one last time, the way his arms had tightened around her. She also remembered the pain in
his eyes and knew it was because of her. With a
muttered exclamation, she shoved the papers to the
floor and glared at them, as if they were somehow
to blame for her foul mood.

Without Burke, the future stretched bleakly before her. He'd made her feel whole again. He had
unsnarled the tangle of hurt and abandonment inside
of her, an ache she hadn't even been aware of. And
he had done it effortlessly, naturally, just by loving
her.

It was a healing kind of love, and she'd thrown
it back in his face. She wasn't the woman for him.
Heck, she didn't have time for a man in her life,
least of all a man like Burke, who deserved a
woman who could love him with her full self. It
took every ounce of energy she had just to keep the
ranch going. What right did she have to ask any
man to take on that kind of responsibility?

She sloshed some coffee into a cup and gulped it
down. The liquid burned her throat, but she welcomed the pain. She focused on it, trying to forget
the gnawing emptiness where her heart should have
been.

This was what she wanted. Well, wasn't it? she
asked herself fiercely. She'd sworn she'd never let
a man get inside her life, her heart, and twist her

up the way her father had done with her mother. She didn't intend to trade her independence for the heartache of marriage. Hadn't her parents taught her anything?

No, she didn't intend getting caught in that trap. Only why did she feel so empty now? As if she were letting something precious slip away? The sense of wistfulness startled her. She wasn't lonely.

Uncle Charlie, the ranch, the kids from the res, they were her life. They were all she needed, all she wanted. Somehow though, it was no longer enough.

Burke's fault, she thought, recognizing the unfairness of it and unable to help herself. He'd changed her, made her vulnerable in ways she didn't want to recognize, didn't want to admit.

Scenes from the past echoed across the years. After all these years, she could still see her mother's tear-streaked face after her father had left. Her mother had been a proud woman and had tried to hide her grief from her small daughter, but Cheyenne had heard her crying during the night when she thought no one could hear.

She stopped. *My father*. She said the words aloud and waited for the pain.

Nothing.

She tried it again. Still, nothing. The bitterness she'd carried with her for twenty-three years was gone, along with the pain. Instead she felt only a quiet acceptance. Her father wasn't an evil person. He just hadn't been cut out to have a family. Why hadn't she understood that before?

Oh, her mind had accepted it. But her heart had never been able to deal with it. For twenty-three years, she'd wrestled with the pain, the guilt, and the abandonment. Why now was she able to let go of it? She searched for an answer even while knowing what it was.

Burke.

It all came back to Burke. And Burke was leaving the following week. Leaving because of her.

She scrubbed a hand along her jaw, wondering how she was going to make it through the rest of the day. She didn't dare think about tomorrow. Or all the tomorrows after that.

Unable to sit still any longer, she stood and paced, her pent-up energy finding no release. The only release, she acknowledged, would be found in Burke's arms, in the taste of his lips, in the feel of his arms as they closed around her.

Confronted with a problem, she did what she always did. She headed out to the barn and saddled Taffy. She gave the horse her head. As if sensing Cheyenne's mood, the little mare galloped over the ground, taking the fences with an easy stride that gave Cheyenne the illusion of flying. At last they pulled to a stop at the stand of firs where she and Burke had picnicked.

There, away from everyone, she dismounted and gazed over the grassland. Scrub brush, dried to the color of sage, dotted the sun-baked ground. A lizard slithered across her boot. The sky was a paintbox of color, gaudy against the dun-colored landscape.

The land worked its magic on her as it always did, pulling her into a different world, bidding her to leave all her troubles behind. She gave herself up to the quiet and let the peace settle over her. When she'd absorbed the serenity, the isolation of it, she hunkered down and dug into the ground, picking up a handful of dirt. She lifted it to her nose and inhaled deeply before letting it sift through her fingers.

The land. It didn't change. Generations had lived, fought, and died here. The continuity of life in all its cycles was here. But the thought failed to comfort her as it had in the past. In fact, nothing brought her any relief these days. Work, even her hours with the kids on the weekends, didn't give the satisfaction she'd once found in it. Even the land, land she'd sweated over, bled for, no longer had the power it once had.

Without Burke, nothing was right.

She stayed there until dusk had fallen, the shadows deepening into night. A breeze shivered over her. Taffy whinnied softly.

With one last look at the endless prairie, Cheyenne turned. ''Okay, girl. Let's go home.''

Tears burned in her eyes, but she refused to wipe them away. She wasn't ashamed of them as she once would have been. A breaking heart deserved a few tears. Briefly she wondered whether it was possible to die from a broken heart. The way she was feeling right now, she wasn't going to bet against it.

The only trouble, she acknowledged silently, was that the only person who could cure what ailed her was the one man she couldn't turn to.

Burke struggled to understand Cheyenne's fear as he shaded his eyes against the harsh rays of the sun. Deliberately, he turned his back on the meadow where the deer cavorted like playful children. It was too painful, a reminder of Cheyenne. Instead, he focused his gaze on the range that stretched hundreds of miles in either direction.

He'd offered her everything he had, everything he was. And she'd tossed it back at him, as though it were nothing.

He swore softly. He was making himself sound like some kind of saint. The fact was, he'd give up everything and do it gladly for the chance to spend the rest of his life with her. Because he couldn't imagine spending it any other way.

Burke tried to push her image from his mind but discovered he couldn't do it. She'd looked so lovely the last time he'd seen her, the sun slanting shafts of light in her hair. The picture was burned into his mind. And his heart.

The admission gave him pause. When had he come to the point of needing a woman—a certain woman—more than he needed his next breath?

A knock at the cabin door made him hurry to answer it. Maybe Cheyenne had changed her mind. Maybe . . . But Uncle Charlie stood there. Burke tried—and failed—to hide his disappointment.

"If you came to talk about your niece—"

Charlie shook his head. "You and Smiling Sun have much to discover about each other. Where is the wisdom for me to talk to you?"

There was no answer to that. Burke gestured for him to come inside.

"Have you ever visited a sweat lodge?" Charlie asked.

"I've heard about them."

"My people believe that in there a man can find the truth he seeks."

"What makes you think I'm seeking truth?"

Charlie paid no attention. "We heat it hotter than any man can stand and then heat it some more. That is when the spirits come in and tell us what we need to know. When a man steps out, he can barely stand, much less walk."

"Why do you do it?"

"Entering the sweat lodge washes away the impurities that keep us from seeing clearly." Charlie studied him gravely. "Do you wish to see?" He asked the question as though Burke had a choice.

"When?"

"Tomorrow. We will join the elders of our tribe." He paused. "Smiling Sun is unhappy." He held up a hand when Burke would have defended himself. "My daughter has much strength inside her. Strength is good, but it is not always easy."

The sweat lodge was a loosely built dome of sapling branches woven together, covered completely with blankets and tarps.

Burke was given a blanket to wear over the loose cotton shorts Uncle Charlie had recommended. After shedding his shoes, he inhaled deeply and crawled inside. He braced himself, letting his eyes adjust to the dimness.

One by one, each man crawled into the lodge and found his place in the circle. In the center was a shallow pit, which was quickly filled with large rocks that had been heated to a glowing red in a nearby fire. When the door flap closed, the darkness was complete. The leader poured water on the hot stones, and the steam rose in clouds. The heat nearly knocked Burke over.

"Breathe deeply," Charlie said. "You will find what you are looking for if your heart is open."

Will I? Burke wondered. "Is that a promise?" He regretted the sarcastic words as soon as they were out of his mouth. Charlie seemed not to have noticed, though.

Burke settled himself on the cool earth and waited. *For what?* he wondered.

He couldn't see the others. With the exception of himself and a young boy whom Charlie had told him was going through a tribal rite of passage, the men were sixty and over. With each splash of the water, they silently endured the rising heat.

"When do I start getting all this wisdom?" Burke asked.

Charlie's voice was gently chiding. "You must wait. Listen. Watch."

"You told me I'd find answers here."

"You are impatient. The spirits will not be rushed. They will work in their own time, in their own way. You must first empty your mind of all that plagues it."

Burke gathered the blanket around himself to fend off the scorching steam, willing his body to relax, to adapt to the heat.

"Do not fight it," Charlie cautioned. "Let the heat into you. It will become one with you. Only then can your mind see past the mist."

Someone struck a drum, and the men began singing in their language. Seconds bled into minutes, minutes into hours. Aside from the few instructions Charlie whispered to him, talking was discouraged. When the time came, the men prayed in low tones for what seemed to Burke an eternity. He couldn't understand a word, but the heartfelt praying touched him somehow.

Burke wet his lips, finding even that small gesture exhausting. Just when he was sure he could stand it no longer, he felt the tension inside him start to dissolve. It flowed out of him, leaving his body limp, but his mind at peace. Was this what Uncle Charlie referred to?

Images of Cheyenne, images that he'd tried to banish, appeared. Colors and scents, as vivid as those of the Wyoming sky at sunset, rolled through his mind.

At the end of about four hours, he staggered out. The fresh air chilled his skin, and he shivered. His muscles tingled with the effects of the heat. He was no nearer to finding the answer he sought than he had been before he'd entered the sweat lodge, though.

"The spirits do not always answer as we expect," Charlie said, apparently sensing Burke's disappointment. He pointed to the sky. "You see the cloud?"

Frustrated, Burke let his gaze follow Charlie's finger and squinted past the sun's glare. He wasn't in the mood for any more of Charlie's mumbo jumbo about spirits and sweat lodges. "It looks like a bear. So what?"

Charlie gave him an approving nod. "Native Americans believe that bears are warriors. And that warriors protect their villages."

So they were back to warriors again. "What does that have to do with me?"

"The answer must come from inside you." Charlie patted Burke's shoulder. "The sweat lodge is only a place where the spirits can talk to you. It is up to you to listen." He pressed a steaming cup into Burke's hands. "Drink."

Burke eyed the brew warily. "What is it?"

"Tea. Chicory and corn silk." Charlie's eyes twinkled. "If you cannot drink it, you can always bathe in it." He took off, his pace that of a much younger man.

Burke could only watch in amazement. Charlie, at seventy-something, had spent the same four hours in the sweat lodge that Burke had, yet he walked with the springy step and squared shoulders of a

young man. Burke estimated that it would be another hour at least before he could move easily
again.

He headed on foot to the ridge rimming the
meadow. He remembered when Cheyenne had
taken him there.

She'd been beautiful that day, her face flushed
from excitement, her hair as shiny as a raven's wing
under the sun. He loved her, always would.

He'd thought he understood pain. But not until
now, until Cheyenne had ordered him out of her
life, did he fully understand what it could do to a
man. Or a woman. Is that what Cheyenne felt when
her father abandoned her? This wrenching feeling
of loss?

Everything he'd ever wanted could have been his.
It had been close enough that he'd believed it within
reach. So close, but not close enough, he thought.
Not close enough.

He glanced toward the ranch. She was there.
Probably mending fence. She'd tackle it with her
customary efficiency and competence, just as she
did any of the hundred other chores that had to be
done to keep a place the size of hers going.

He thought about it. One woman from now
throughout the rest of his life. Responsibility. Permanence. Devotion. At one time, the idea would

have terrified him, sent him running in the other direction as fast as his legs could carry him.

Now it thrilled him on a level deeper than he'd ever expected he was capable of.

He could still walk away. She wouldn't blame him for it. In fact, she probably expected it. He wondered who had left her besides her father. His lips tightened at the idea that she'd been hurt by another man. He'd make it up to her, he vowed.

In the heat of late September, the land was hard and unyielding. Desert yellow, it could be cruel, exacting a price from those not experienced in its ways, not willing to bend to its demands.

But it was also magnificent. Its stark beauty pulled at him just as it had that first day. As he climbed, the air seemed fresher, clearer. Traveler must have sensed the difference too for he whickered. Burke patted his neck.

It grew cooler until at last they were picking their way over the rocky ridge that rimmed the meadow. Here, the land, fed by a small spring, blossomed with color. A shrill trumpeting from a bull moose made him stand in the stirrups, straining to see in the distance.

The herd of animals was as beautiful as the land. He belonged here.

''I belong here.'' He laughed.

This was his home.

And if Cheyenne couldn't see that, then it was up to him to convince her of it. He'd never been a quitter before. He didn't intend to start now.

Cheyenne was just going to have to accept it. He was here to stay. She loved him. And he loved her. It was up to him to make her see it. The heaviness that had settled around his heart for the last week lifted.

Back in the cabin, he understood he had a choice to make. He could take Cheyenne at her word and pack up and leave. Or he could stay and convince her that he loved her and they belonged together.

Passionate. Committed. Fiercely loyal. She was all those things. And more. Uncle Charlie was right. She would never be easy. What the heck. Most things worth having weren't. He stood and straightened his shoulders. The lady had a few home truths coming. And he was just the one to deliver them.

Chapter Nine

Her head heavy and aching, Cheyenne forced herself out of bed. She'd spent too many days moping around feeling sorry for herself. She intended on changing that.

Starting now.

Sleep had eluded her for the past week. If she was lucky, she managed to snatch a few hours near morning when her exhausted mind and bruised heart finally gave up the struggle and succumbed to the oblivion of sleep.

Inevitably, she awoke to the depressing memory that nothing had changed. Burke was leaving. And she was letting him go. She had no choice, she reminded herself. The only other alternative was to admit that she loved him. And that she could not do.

Could not or would not?

She pushed the thought away, headed for the shower, and tried to remember what it had felt like to be happy. She had an uneasy feeling that memories of the feeling might be all she had to look forward to in the future.

Though she'd told Uncle Charlie dozens of times in the past not to bother fixing breakfast for her, Charlie had made fried bread. Cheyenne forced a smile to her lips while groaning inwardly. The last thing she felt like doing was eating. Dutifully, though, she pushed the food around on her plate, aware that she wasn't fooling her uncle.

''That was great,'' Cheyenne said as she started out the door.

Rather than the scolding she expected, Uncle Charlie gave her a sympathetic look, which had the effect of making her feel worse than ever. She headed outside. A breeze stirred the air, and she inhaled deeply.

She lifted her gaze to study the horizon. Pink and orange streaked the sky, a vivid contrast to the brown of the scorched earth. Sunrise was her favorite time of day. Then, with the air still retaining a hint of the night's chill and the heat of the day only a promise, she could believe in dreams.

Burke believed in dreams; he even had her *wanting* to believe. She allowed herself a small smile. Since when had she started believing in dreams?

Dreams.

Burke.

The two went together.

What had he said about her dream of turning Sweet Water into a full-time place for children with physical and mental disabilities? A frown puckered her brow as she tried to remember.

If you want something hard enough, you'll make it happen.

Well, she wanted it.

You have to say it aloud.

Feeling foolish, she said the words. "I want to turn the ranch into a full-time place for children with disabilities." She repeated the words.

Something stirred inside her—a quickening of excitement that made her believe she could make her dream come true. If she did, she'd have Burke to thank.

Burke believed in dreams, just as he believed in love.

Love.

The word she'd shied away from for so many years. The word that Burke had needed her to say. The word she couldn't say.

So what was she left with?

Nothing. She tried reminding herself that that's what she'd had before he found his way into her life, but the emptiness she experienced now was that much more painful because she knew what fulfillment felt like.

She shook her head in derision. Here she was thinking about dreams. Well, dreams weren't going to mend the fence or anything else. Work waited for her, but she found no pleasure in the thought. She started to the barn where Traveler greeted her with a loud snort. Burke had returned Traveler to the ranch yesterday when she'd been out.

Cheyenne scratched the big gelding behind the ears. ''You miss him, don't you?''

Traveler snorted again. He needed exercise, so she decided to take him instead of Taffy. ''Come on, boy, we've got work to do.'' She spared a moment to pet the little mare. ''I'll bring you a treat when I get back,'' she promised.

The lightning storm that had cost Cheyenne her barn had never produced the promised rain. With a practiced eye, she scanned the sky. A darkening of the clouds gave her pause.

She found Hank and Quinn already on the job. If they noticed that Cheyenne wasn't giving full attention to her work, they didn't say. Neither did they mention that her temper was hot enough to light fireworks, or that her smiles were in short supply.

No, no one said a thing. They treated her with an annoying deference, as though she were sick. And she was, she admitted, sick at heart. That she had no one to blame for it but herself did nothing to improve her temper or her disposition.

Well, all that was going to change. Cheyenne Roberts had always held up her side of the job. That wasn't going to change because of some man. She shrugged off her vest and started to work.

His declaration of love was only so many words. Hadn't her father said the same thing to her mother? Promising to love her forever, he'd stuck it out barely six years. And the love he'd vowed had deteriorated long before he'd walked out. No, she wouldn't make the same mistake her mother made of believing a man's promises.

She had a full, satisfying life. She had her independence. She had much more than many women. What more could she want?

A husband. Children. Family.

The answer came so forcefully that she couldn't deny the truth of it.

Cheyenne tossed a bale of hay over the side of the truck, working alongside Hank and Quinn as they threw out feed for the cattle they'd left in a high meadow. The work was backbreaking and grueling. She spared a moment to wet down her kerchief with water from her canteen and then wrapped it around her neck, sighing in pleasure at the blessed coolness.

The wind would dry her skin off soon enough, but the cool cloth afforded a few minutes of relief. That's all a body could ask for when the temperature climbed into the high nineties. The weather took its own sweet time catching up with the calendar, she thought. And it could change without notice.

She snapped out an order to get back to work when she caught Hank and Quinn giving her guarded looks.

It was only a matter of time before one or both of them called her on it. That Hank chose today when her temper was already on a short fuse was just plain bad luck.

''Boss?''

Cheyenne looked up from the pitchfork resting in her hand to see Hank shuffling from foot to foot, a sign he was itching to tell her something she didn't want to hear. ''Yeah?''

Hank tugged at his kerchief as if it were suddenly too tight for his neck. ''Me and Quinn . . . we've been talking.''

Cheyenne waited.

''We . . . uh . . . think you ought to get back together with the Kincaid feller. For a city boy, he weren't half bad.''

She'd been right. She didn't like it. "You do, do you?"

Hank cleared his throat. "Yeah. We do." He made a sputtering sound and then spat out a stream of tobacco juice. "You've been as cantankerous as a moose without its mate ever since the two of you broke up."

"We didn't break up—" She broke off. She wasn't about to explain herself.

"We . . . uh . . . just noticed you seemed a heap happier when you and he was keeping company." He tipped his hat. "I'd better be getting back to work.

Taking pity on him, Cheyenne said, "Yeah. You'd better." She watched her friend take himself off and turned back to her own work. She pushed herself until her muscles wept with fatigue. When they took a break for lunch, she continued until the job was complete. Exhaustion demanded that she take a break, but if she stopped, if she gave in to the weariness that dogged her, she'd have time to think, to remember, to feel.

She rode back to the barn to pick up fencing supplies. Mending fence was a never-ending chore. She might as well get to it.

An hour into the job hadn't improved her mood. She muttered something under her breath as she set a staple in the fence post. She tipped her hat back and scanned the sky. She turned back to her work and sighed. Just a couple more to go and she'd be done.

By the end of the day, she was filthy and bone-sore. But the activity had accomplished its purpose. She was too tired to think, too tired to worry, too tired to do anything but take a shower and fall into bed.

She was paying for it the following morning. Her injured leg had started to throb again. Uncle Charlie was waiting for her as she limped into the kitchen.

She pasted on a smile that felt as false as the makeup she'd used to hide the ravages of too many sleepless nights.

''You are not my Smiling Sun today,'' he said with his customary bluntness.

She'd thought she might manage to convince him that she was all right. She should have known she couldn't fool him.

''You work with the energy of six horses, but it cannot ease the pain in your heart.''

She forced a laugh. ''My heart is fine. It's yours I worry about.''

''My heart is whole. Yours weeps for the Rainbow Warrior.''

''Burke isn't the Rainbow Warrior.'' She might as well have saved her breath.

''You love him.''

"Did the spirits tell you that?" she asked.

He shook his head. "The spirits do not tell us what is plain for all to see."

"You think I love Burke? You're wrong." Her voice was calm, she was pleased to note. Not a hitch or a quiver in it.

"I have seen how you look at him. You wear your heart in your eyes. You love him. The only one who does not know it is you."

Cheyenne didn't bother correcting her uncle. She wasn't in love with Burke. Sure, she cared about him. She respected him. She even liked him. But love? No way. She wasn't about to get caught in that trap. Love wasn't in the cards for her. It never had been.

"Love is not to be feared."

"I don't—"

Uncle Charlie reproached her with his eyes. "You have never spoken less than the truth to me. Will you start now?"

Chastened, she bowed her head. "No. I won't."

"Good." He pressed her head against his shoulder.

She stayed there for long moments, drinking in the peace she found with his arms around her.

"Pride is a foolish man's burden." He waited a beat. "And a woman's."

She was surprised she could smile. ''You always did say I had my share of pride.''

''Pride keeps you from seeking the happiness you yearn for. You are in danger of losing one who loves you.'' Uncle Charlie tapped his heart. ''You think with your mind. Sometimes you must think with your heart. The Rainbow Warrior loves you. And you return that love.''

''He's not the Rainbow Warrior,'' she said. ''He's just a man.''

''A man who loves you.''

Cheyenne's expression hardened. She tried to convince herself that her heart did the same. ''That's the kind of thinking Mama did. And look where it got her.''

''You are a fool, Daughter. You disappoint me.''

That stung. It was the harshest thing her uncle had ever said to her. She blinked back tears. ''I'm sorry I've disappointed you.''

''You disappoint yourself.''

She spun around. ''I can't. Don't you understand? I can't love him.''

''It is too late. You already do.''

Her anger drained from her. With a swipe at her eyes, she turned her back to him, unwilling for him to see her cry.

Gently, he turned her to face him. ''The man is a true warrior. He would not desert you. I have taught you how to search for truth, how to know it from that which would deceive you. Have I not?''

''Yes, Uncle. You have.''

He nodded in acceptance. ''Now you must look for it within your heart.''

''What are you talking about?''

''Love, Daughter. It is there in his eyes when he looks at you.'' He shook his head, his eyes sad. ''I have never seen you afraid. Until now.

''It is time you looked within yourself.'' He handed her a sack lunch. ''Go. Find the peace you seek. Then we will talk.''

She kissed him on the cheek and took off.

Cheyenne rode to the ridge overlooking the meadow where she'd taken Burke. She watched two deer, a doe and her fawn, walk quietly out of the forest to drink from the sluggish creek, their delicate legs lost in the low-lying mist that layered the ground. Content, she remained hidden, hoping the deer would not catch her scent. The scene, as peaceful as the lazy clouds that scudded across the sky, soothed her troubled heart.

It invoked memories from her first hunting trip with Uncle Charlie. They'd been looking for deer. It was black powder season, and she'd been anxious to bring home her first buck.

Even at twelve, Cheyenne had understood the significance of being taken along on a hunt. Uncle

Charlie had impressed upon her from the beginning that taking a life carried with it responsibilities. Only hunt for food, and take only what you can use. No more, no less. Those rules were as ingrained in her as that of never wasting water. They were simply one more part of making a living from the land.

They'd spent two hours without coming across so much as a sign of a deer.

"It's a waste of time," Cheyenne had complained.

Uncle Charlie's wise eyes had smiled down at her. "Animals do not let us see them until they want us to see them. It's the hunter's job to convince them to remove the blindfold from our eyes. You must call out to the deer and listen to what he says. The animals will let us know when they are ready to be seen."

Within the next hour, they had two bucks in their sights, but Uncle Charlie had lowered his rifle and gestured for her to do the same.

Incensed, she'd turned on him.

"It was not their time," her uncle had said. "Listen. They say that they are not ready, that another will come in their place."

"How will I know?"

"You will know," he promised. "If you listen with your eyes."

She didn't understand, but she nodded.

When another buck, a six prong, appeared, her uncle nodded. ''He says, 'It's a good day to die.' '' His words rushed back to her now.

It had been her first hunt, her first kill. A country girl, she wasn't naive enough to believe that meat appeared in the supermarket neatly wrapped in tidy packages.

She'd butchered her share of cows and sheep and pigs. She didn't like it, doubted she'd ever like it, but she'd done it because it had to be done. Dying was as much a part of nature's cycle as was living. She accepted it. And knew she lost part of her childhood with each slaughtering.

Her uncle had her do the butchering of the deer as well. The gruesome process was backbreaking and took more guts than she thought she possessed, but she'd made it and had returned home with both meat for the family and pride in her skill. But she hadn't gone hunting again for three more years. Uncle Charlie had understood.

Looking back, she'd realized that it had been but one more of his subtle lessons.

When restlessness pushed her to action, she tracked a buck, enjoying the rush of adrenaline at the hunt. She had no intention of shooting. Her only objective now was to watch and admire.

It was a beautiful place, a place to dream dreams . . . a place to find love.

And she had.

The memory caused her throat to tighten. She thrust it away before the tears could start again. She'd wasted enough time crying. She'd have a life-time of regrets. She didn't need to dwell on them now.

She lifted her gaze to study the gathering clouds. It was going to storm. She remembered another time, another storm. And the fire. Burke had fought his way into the barn to rescue her and the horses.

The rain, so long awaited, started as she returned home, gentle drops at first, then great gushing cur-rents of it. She took off her hat and lifted her face to the sky, letting the rain soak her hair and skin.

Uncle Charlie was waiting for her when she walked inside, cold, wet, and shivering. He took one look at her and told her he'd have soup ready for her after she'd changed into dry clothes. "Then we will talk."

A hot shower banished the goosebumps that puckered her flesh. She stalled as long as she could before going downstairs. She knew he planned to finish the conversation they'd started this morning.

"Did you find the peace you sought?" he asked after she had put down a bowl of bean soup, thick with vegetables and bacon.

She hadn't known real peace since she'd watched

Burke ride away. ''There is peace in my work,'' she said at last.

A glance at her uncle's face told her she hadn't fooled him a bit.

Uncle Charlie said a word she rarely heard him use. ''You love him. You lied to Burke. You can lie to me. But do not lie to yourself.''

''I'm not lying—'' Cheyenne stopped. She looked at her hands, dismayed to find that they were shaking. She curled them at her sides in an attempt to control their trembling. And to hide them from her uncle who saw too much. ''It's too late,'' she said at last, finally stuffing her hands inside her pockets.

''You love him,'' he repeated.

Cheyenne wanted to deny it, meant to, but the protest died on her lips. ''I love him.''

The words came with such ease that she wondered how she hadn't realized it before. She loved him. She loved Burke. Of course. That's why she'd fought so long and hard against her feelings for him. That's why she'd failed to understand her attraction to him. Love had been so lacking in her life that she didn't recognize it even when it was staring her in the face.

She wanted it and all that went with it—home, a real one, marriage, family, routine—with the surprises children always provided thrown in for good measure.

She blew air through her teeth. At one time, she'd have scorned such a dream. Now it felt right. Because she'd found the right man.

Everything was simple now. She'd find him, tell him that she loved him and . . . She shook her head, remembering that he was due to leave tomorrow. She looked out the window to find the sun low in the sky. "He's leaving."

Uncle Charlie nodded. "What will you do about it?"

For the first time in a week, Cheyenne smiled. It felt good. "Stop him." She kissed her uncle's cheek. "Wish me luck."

"The spirits have smiled on you. That is all the luck you will need."

"I love you," Cheyenne called over her shoulder. She glanced back to see her uncle smiling widely.

She saddled Taffy, her normally smooth movements jerky and impatient. "Come on, girl. We've got to find the Rainbow Warrior."

She reveled in the feel of the rain-chilled wind whipping her hair across her face as she and Traveler raced across the prairie. Freedom—it was there in the wind, the land, the mountains. But she'd failed to see it before. She'd seen the responsibility, the legacy, the duty, but never the freedom.

Without the walls she'd erected around herself, she could feel it. Happiness awaited her. All that she had to do was reach out and grab it. That, she thought, and convince Burke to accept that she loved him. First she had to find him. She didn't let herself think about what would happen after that.

She headed to the cabin. She stepped gingerly around pockets of muddy water that dotted the rough ground.

It was beautiful. The land never failed to arouse a strong feeling of connectedness within her. She'd felt it years ago as a child. She felt it now.

The cabin was empty.

She hadn't known she could hurt like this, a stab of pain lancing straight to the heart. She made a low, keening sound, like an animal in pain, as she felt her heart being torn out.

When she took the time to look around, she noticed that some of his belongings were still there. Maybe he hadn't left for good. Maybe there was still a chance.

She held onto that hope as she rode as fast as the darkening sky allowed. At home, she stuffed her saddlebags with what she needed, called to Uncle Charlie not to wait up, and started back to the cabin.

She filled the room with candles. Fat ones. Skinny ones. Tall ones. Short ones. Scented and unscented. Their fragrance wafted through the room, pleasing her with the welcome they offered. She placed five in each window, an unmistakable symbol, she hoped.

There was but one last detail. She set the wedding vase, filled with wildflowers, on the table.

Suddenly unsure of herself, she pushed the door open and scanned the dusk-softened landscape. When would he be here? Would he even come back? The questions taunted her and the risk she'd taken. She'd bared her heart just by being here.

Whatever happened between her and Burke, she'd have the satisfaction of knowing she'd fought for him. But was she too late?

A call from his boss had caused Burke to leave the day before and make the twelve-hour trip to Denver. He'd come up with all the answers, made the right noises, and was pathetically grateful when it was over.

He was glad to be out of the city and back on the road toward home.

Rain that had stubbornly evaded Wyoming now fell in sheets over the plains. Puddles shimmered beneath the glare of his headlights, splattering the undersides of his truck. Though anxious to get home—that was how he thought of the cabin now— he kept the speed down. A slick road made driving treacherous. He turned the windshield wipers on high, the incessant swish-swish a counterpoint to his tangled thoughts.

The landscape glistened with moisture. He was fiercely glad for Cheyenne's sake that the land was getting the rain it needed. She was probably out dancing in it, he thought with a slight smile. Dancing and rejoicing. Well, she deserved to celebrate. He knew what the rain meant to the area ranchers and farmers.

He pulled into the rough road leading to the cabin just past dusk. His truck bumped along the pitted track until he brought it to an abrupt stop.

Candles.

They lit up the cabin like a Christmas tree. His mind flicked through the possibilities. A transient looking for a place to spend the night? A lost camper? He rejected each in turn.

His heart gave a hitch, then started to race. *Cheyenne?* Was it possible? He pulled the truck to a stop and was running. At the door, he stopped. What if she'd come to tell him good-bye and planned this as some kind of farewell?

Dozens of candles filled the room. On the table sat the wedding vase, a profusion of wildflowers overflowing in it.

He found her on the narrow bed, her hair curtaining her face. She looked much as she had the first time he'd seen her. And as it had been that first time, his heart stopped. He stared and let his eyes savor the sight of her.

When he couldn't keep his hands to himself any longer, he bent to brush her hair from her face and place a kiss on her lips. ''Sleeping Beauty,'' he whispered.

She stirred, murmuring something he couldn't make out, then jerked awake, her eyes widening. She scrambled off the bed and stood.

He searched for something to say and settled for ''Hi.'' *Good going, Kincaid. Can't you think of anything more original than that?*

''Hi.'' Her voice betrayed nerves. The knowledge steadied his own.

''The candles. They're nice.''

''Thanks.''

He resisted the temptation to take her in his arms. If she came to him, it had to be because *she* wanted it.

''Why?'' he asked. ''Why did you come?'' He wanted to hear the words. *Needed* to hear them.

''Because I don't want you to go.''

''Why?''

''I love you.''

He marveled at the sound of the words on her lips. She'd shunned them, he knew, afraid of what they'd mean if she dared utter them aloud. Now, they fell off her tongue with an ease that amazed him, and, he expected, her.

''Don't say it if you don't mean it,'' Burke said in a tight voice. ''I couldn't stand it.''

''I've never said anything I don't mean. I don't intend to start now. I've been doing a lot of thinking. There're no guarantees. No absolutes. Except one.''

''What's that?''

''This.'' She stood on tiptoe and pressed a kiss to his lips. ''I love you. Whatever happens, that won't change. That won't ever change.''

She looked at him, her gaze searching his face.

''You love me.'' He said the words slowly, testing them, hearing the truth in them.

''I have for a long time. I just didn't want to admit it.''

''What made you change your mind?''

''It wasn't a question of changing my mind. It was . . .'' She paused. ''I was afraid.''

''Of me?''

''Of loving you.'' She drew a deep breath. ''Of loving anyone. I kept remembering my parents. They loved each other. Once. But it died and left something ugly and bitter in its place. For a long time, too long, I couldn't see beyond that. My father—''

"Didn't know what he was giving up. It wasn't your fault." It wasn't your fault," he repeated.

"I know that. Now." She turned her face in his palm. "You helped me see that."

He shook her head. "I didn't do anything."

"But you did. You loved me. Even when I tried to push you away, you kept right on loving me."

"I didn't have any choice in the matter."

"Neither do I." She kissed him and then lifted a hand to cup his cheek. "We're not my parents."

He caught her hand and brought it to his lips, drawing her to him at the same time. "No. We're not."

"We're us—you and me."

"That's all we need." He threw her a teasing look. "I'd made up my mind to stay. I was going to convince you that you loved me even if it took the rest of my life. I'm glad it's not going to take that long."

"Not half as glad as I am."

"I've been thinking about your plans to turn the ranch into a full-time place for children with disabilities."

"It's hardly a plan. Only a dream. Maybe . . . someday."

"I told you once that I believe in dreams."

"I remember."

"Have you ever thought of taking on a partner?"

"It'd be great. The problem is no one would be willing to work for what I can afford to pay."

"I wouldn't be so sure about that. It ought to be someone who shares your dream. Someone to work toward it with you. Someone who can help with the kids and the horses."

She was beginning to understand. A slow smile played across her lips. "Did you have anyone in mind?"

"As a matter of fact, I do. Me."

"You'd do that?"

"All you have to do is ask."

"But your job . . . I can't ask you to give it up. That's your dream."

"You're not asking. And I can keep my job. I talked it over with my boss while I was in Denver." Gently, he fit his finger at the part of her lips. "I want to help make your dream come true. If you'll let me."

She looked at him, afraid to believe what she was hearing. He'd given her so much already. How could she ask for more? But the love she saw shining in his eyes confirmed that she'd heard correctly.

"Our dream," she corrected softly. "Yours and mine."

He must have understood what she was saying

for he brought her hand to his cheek. ''We'll make it come true, Cheyenne. We can do it. Anything's possible . . . as long as we're together.''

With Burke at her side, she could do anything. Love surged through her. ''Together.''